Sage and Sweetgrass

LoRee Peery

Sage and Sweetgrass

Contact Information: titleadmin@pelicanbookgroup.com

Cover Art by *Artist Nicola Martinez*

White Rose Publishing, a division of Pelican Ventures, LLC
www.whiterosepublishing.com PO Box 1738 *Aztec, NM * 87410

White Rose Publishing Circle and Rosebud logo is a trademark of Pelican Ventures, LLC

Publishing History
First White Rose Edition, 2012
Print Edition ISBN 978-1-61116-097-0
Electronic Edition ISBN 978-1-61116-098-7
Published in the United States of America

Dedication

Dedicated to my sister, Renée Mosel, whose bravery humbles me.

To my brother, Gaylen Mosel, an artist and horse whisperer, sage in his own unique way.

And to every reader: I hope you know the Lord has His hand on your life.

Also Available

Frivolities Series

Moselle's Insurance
Rainn on My Parade

1

I am alive...

Somewhere out there, is someone waiting to share my life?

"Somewhere out there," Lanae Petersen sang. "That's the snippet I wrote when I journaled this morning." Her sing-song statement elicited a wide grin from her sister, Geneva Carson.

"I'm thankful you found that journal writing such a help while you were sick," Geneva commented.

The little catch phrases or quotes Lanae had latched onto after she found out hepatitis C was the cause of her sickness, were the only things that got her through some days.

And reading the Bible, of course.

Lanae glanced at the art-glass design of the sun catcher hanging in the window, a gift from Rainn Harris, Geneva's fiancé. She compared the pattern with the appliqué cross Geneva was now anchoring onto the background fabric of her current wall quilt.

"I suspect your latest project isn't meant as a shop item but as a gift for Rainn."

"You got it." Geneva lifted her brows to see above the rim of her glasses. "I can't get over how different you are from a couple months ago. Look at you now, pouring over those singles ads."

"I'm alive. Praise God." Lanae slapped the newspaper against her lap and waved her open arms toward the ceiling.

Geneva shook her head, an indulgent smile spreading across her face.

"But for God's grace, I could still be caught up in that nightmare illness. I used to wonder if I would ever feel alive or die too sick to enjoy the life I have," Lanae said. She dropped her arms and picked up the paper. Running her finger down a bolded column, she read out loud, "'Men Seeking.' I feel all crocheted out and full of the energy I didn't have while I was sick. We may have opened *Frivolities*, but a lot of it I don't remember. I feel like I slept through it."

Geneva shared a look that took them back to girlhood.

Thank you, Lord, for the comfort I've found in words. And thank You for my sister. Lanae turned back to her newspaper reading. "This guy wants nice legs. I have those...Mmmm, here's a cowboy."

"Do any say if they're Christian?" Geneva asked around the needle between her lips as she measured a length of thread.

"Not yet. Here's an SWM, Single White Male, looking for smarts. Ohhkaaay. I might give this one an answer. He's a ranch owner." Mourning what could have been, Lanae rubbed a spot of newspaper dust off the soft dark leather of her recliner. A life lived out on her own ranch. "Then again, been there, done that, with my rancher." *But he died before the culmination of their life together.* Lanae contemplated the word "dream," sighed over the memory of her deceased husband, and formed a sad smile. The Lord's timing had no explanation.

Their shop, *Frivolities*, was the widowed sisters' joint business venture. When she'd seen the ad in their hometown paper listing a downtown building for sale in Platteville, she jumped at the chance to move back to where she'd been born. Geneva called Lanae in response to the same ad. *Certainly seemed like God's prompting.*

"Remember, it was an ad that helped bring *Frivolities* into existence," Lanae emphasized. "Look, this one says he'll treat you like a lady. Oh boy. A Western lover—books and movies."

"Gotta be a touch of country there."

Lanae loved wide open spaces. She had tried to keep her husband Keith's dream ranch alive after his death. It had slammed into her one day, the sad realization that she no longer had the resources to stick with the ranch. How she missed the expanse. "'I'm your dream come true if you love nature and horses.' This sounds good." Lanae glanced at her sister. "He says he likes gospel music."

Geneva laid the colorful fabric in her lap and gave Lanae a look as sharp as the needle she used to accent the appliquéd edges. "You aren't really going to jump on this bandwagon by answering one of those ads, are you?"

"Thinking about it. It's better than taking a chance on one of those dot-com sites, to my way of thinking." Lanae continued to skim the column. "Oh joy. This guy wants a woman to believe in him...and finally, it says he believes in Jesus. Can't buy it, though. He also lists his astrological sign."

"There you go. Satan believes in Jesus, too."

Lanae sighed. Jesus held her future the same as He'd been with her all her life.

"And speaking of ads..." she brushed her fingers to the side.

"Find someone interesting?"

"Across the page here is a little something that would fit in the shop. Listen to this. 'Oak dressing table. Needs refinishing. Solid. Original glass pulls on fancy drawers. Make offer.'" She raised a brow and met her sister's glance. "Looks like a Lincoln phone number."

"Want to check it out in the morning? Beth will be working in the shop for Moselle. If you have a cheesecake ready tonight, you'd be free to drive down to Lincoln in the morning."

"Think I'll give them a call later," Lanae said as she once again buried her nose in the paper.

Besides the gifts, antiques, and frivolities the shop sold, they had an espresso machine and Lanae's baked goods. Customers came in and experienced...no, savored, their offerings. It was a God-thing, how the idea for the crazy items—Moselle's handcrafts, Geneva's quilts and specialty coffees, and Lanae's crochet and cheesecakes—had come to them at the same time when they'd each seen the building advertised. With the long state of Nebraska between them, each sister had recognized the opportunity to use her skills for profit.

She considered the *Frivolities* women. At the moment, her niece Moselle—the third party in the *Frivolities* venture—was on her honeymoon, or she'd be working on a craft designed from old items right along with them. Mondays, when the shop was closed, weren't always for leisure. It was their practice to meet as part of their business plan and to work on their contributions to keep *Frivolities* stocked with goodies.

"They must bold these ads with large print so oldies like me can read 'em."

"Yeah, right. You think we're old in our fifties? Aren't you the one who told me we're only as old as we think we are?"

The sisters shared a look that covered a myriad of unspoken thoughts.

"You could find yourself a man. After all, I found my Rainn. That way your guy could do the reading when your eyes go." Geneva's teasing held a dreamy quality.

"If my eyes go, I'll blame it on all that crocheting I did instead of sleeping when I was sick." Lanae flipped the page to see how many more columns the ads covered. None. The singles were confined to one page.

She studied her sister. Geneva looked so pretty in love. She could almost pass for her daughter, Moselle.

"I agree. You got yourself one in a million with your Rainn, my dear Geneva. Like the Elvis quote I read the other day that says we're meant to do something worth remembering. You've sure done that with that sweet man of yours." Lanae drummed her fingers on the paper in her lap. "I believe I am ready to seek my own man, to do my own something-worth-remembering."

"Wait a minute, here." Geneva set her elbow against her hip bone, needle pointed in the air, and gave Lanae a get-real look. "You were married to a Vietnam vet. You held onto the ranch over twenty years after Keith died. I'd call that doing something worth remembering."

"Guess you're right. Not to mention creating *Frivolities* with you. Now that I'm feeling alive again, it might be nice to seriously search for a man of my own.

To warm my winter nights, you know...someone to share it all with."

"Have to admit, those strong arms of Rainn's help me feel tucked in safe and warm every night."

"That sounds interesting. You mean he moved in when I moved out of your house?" Lanae snorted.

"Not funny. Rainn and I say good night even if it's by phone. And if he's at the scene of a fire, I have Mia to attend to. So I'm not alone."

"That girl. Remember how she spelled out her name and pronounced it 'M-E-ah,' so we'd all get it right?" They shared reminiscent smiles.

Mia's mother, Rainn's sister, was a single mom who died of drug-related, mysterious circumstances in Fort Worth, Texas. Rainn's parents wanted no part of caring for a child with special needs; so Rainn became custodial caregiver of his six-year-old niece, a special child with autism.

Lanae shook her head and shot another smile at Geneva. She was still trying to wrap her mind around the vast changes in their family over the last few months.

First, her niece, Moselle, had reunited with her high school love, Eric, and married him seventy-two hours ago, the day after Thanksgiving.

Second, Geneva had blossomed every day because of the attention Rainn Harris, Eric's firefighter buddy, paid her. He'd rescued her from a tree, where she'd climbed after a stray cat. The family still made jokes about it, how she'd fallen into his arms when he rescued her.

Third, Lanae had overcome hep C. "You and I got used to sleeping single in a double bed, Sis. Now I'm going to try with all my might to see if that's really

God's plan for the rest of my life."

"You may very well have a point. He spared you from a terminal illness." The smile accompanying Geneva's words brought the blessing home. "But don't get too carried away with your own plan instead of waiting on the Lord."

Lanae shot up a silent prayer of thankfulness for her healthy liver and went back to reading the ads out loud. "Here's one. 'Integrity and full of heart.' Meaning, no heart disease, I'll wager." She emitted a throaty, scoffing sound. "Oooh, this one sounds like me. 'Country boy at heart, but caught in town.'"

"If that doesn't sound like you, I'll eat my needle," Geneva mumbled around that sharp object.

"Don't laugh, or you just might," Lanae said. Then she laughed loud enough for both of them.

This particular Monday morning's working session and business meeting had fizzled. Wedding and holiday still filled the atmosphere, so Geneva and Lanae had made short business of their shop-talk duties. They now attended to the creative side of their joint venture, working on individual quilted fabric and crochet items.

Well, Lanae had attempted to work. She'd eventually set aside her crochet hook and picked up the newspaper.

The women closest to Lanae, sister and niece, faced the future with their respective firefighters. The men had their softer sides. Eric sold insurance and built birdhouses for fun. Rainn was a stained glass artist and would soon start teaching at community college.

Dare Lanae follow through with her planned man hunt?

Lord willing.

She had been content with her life. She hadn't faced the loneliness, or missed having a man around, until she witnessed what love did for the two women she loved.

She missed the poignancy of love, how much brighter and happier life could be when shared with the right person. But she was a different person now, living in a different time and place. Maybe God had a new plan for her. But if this was it, she would be happy as long as she followed God's will.

Lanae glanced out the sliding glass door and followed the trail of a dancing cottonwood leaf as it drifted to the ground. "But you know, sis, I really do miss it at times. The ranch. Those open miles where the sun causes a gal to crinkle and wrinkle. The meadowlarks and bugs and wind in my hair."

"What hair?"

"Very funny."

The memory of hair loss sobered Lanae. Her Hep C meds hadn't caused her to lose hers like some cancer treatments did, but her hair sure had thinned. She'd decided to keep her hair short.

Joy and peace now flushed her soul.

She ran her fingertips over the leather chair that offered comfort every time the deep cushions welcomed her. Family and friends had taken up a collection for the recliner, and a grand gift it was. She'd been so overwhelmed with their outpouring of love.

But was the love of God, family, and friends enough for fulfilling relationships? Or was she meant to find a special someone to spend the rest of her days with?

Lanae's gaze traced the blocks in the quilt Geneva

had made, which now graced the wall. Arranged in varied blocks of crosses, surrounding one huge cross in front of a blazing gold light, the teal and mauve colors never failed to warm her heart. The thick quilt had warded off the chill on her legs, originally serving the purpose of lap blanket.

Should she be looking for someone? Or should she leave it to God to bring that special someone to her?

Or, should she, like the biblical Paul, be content with what she had?

Lanae played with the strap of the denim bag Moselle had designed. The tote was created from a pair of old jeans. Lanae tucked away her balls of yarn and current crochet project into the bag.

"I would imagine Moselle and Eric are having a great time about now." Geneva spoke on a wistful sigh as though wishing she was on her own honeymoon.

The sisters exchanged understanding smiles. Lanae's turned into laughter then higher pitched giggles as Geneva's color rose to a deep blush.

Lanae set her tote on a nearby shelf and straightened her journal and daily devotional on the cabinet top. She folded the newspaper in her lap and took in her immediate surroundings.

Eric, her new nephew by marriage, had built the cabinet next to her recliner. Handcrafted in golden oak, the cabinet itself consisted of two shelves and a routed edged top.

The stained-glass sun catcher caught her eye again and she said a prayer of thankfulness for Rainn, her soon-to-be brother-in-law. Sections of amber and pink glass in the shape of a rose formed the backdrop for the amber cross.

Humbled anew at their gifts of love, she realized

yet again how blessed she was to have so many loved ones in her life.

Yet, no special man filled the role of lover.

Lanae slapped her knee with the folded paper and smoothed out the dents. "Onward and upward."

She opened the pages and renewed her perusal of the ads. "'Are you the one for me? Can we be friends first?'"

"A young guy wants an older woman?" Geneva quipped.

"In your dreams," they chorused, caught the other's eye, and giggled.

"Your dream came true," Lanae sassed.

"Lucky me."

"No such thing as luck," they joined voices again; same slight nuance in tone, same inflection, same identical timing.

The sisters shared familial comfort and continued with their individual tasks.

****

Sage Diamond questioned his decision. Was he making a mistake by letting go of his last solid link to family? He ran his hand over the scarred surface of the dresser. It sure looked different from when he was a kid.

He'd sat on the edge of the bed, still as a nose-twitching rabbit, and watched his mother. She'd perch in front of the mirror and select her various cosmetics and creams. He'd studied the female ritual of applying the contents of those curious jars. The process remained a mystery, to his way of thinking.

Once the dresser was sold and gone, there would

be no more tangible pieces of his childhood. His mother was gone. His aunts had died young. And memories of Uncle Ted had been buried for a long time—along with the family secret.

He took a step back. For sure, if the mirror were attached, he didn't think he could say good-bye.

From the depths of repressed memory, he heard his mother sing to him, by way of answering his questions.

"When I was just a little boy, I asked my mother..."

And with every question he fired, she'd smile, ruffle his hair, and then continue to sing the answer. "What will you be when you grow up?"

They'd continue singing back and forth, suggesting occupations.

He'd long ago given up wondering, or wishing, for anything good, for what or who he'd be the rest of his life.

What was so great about life? People you love die and leave you alone.

He sure never dreamt he'd be a young widower.

How could he have imagined that he'd have a daughter who became a mother as a teen and a grandson whose father was a mystery?

No time to contemplate life's unsolved issues. He had horses to feed.

****

The first thing Lanae did after Geneva said good night, was to get two cheesecakes in the oven. Then she picked up the phone, curious about the oak vanity.

A nice sounding man with a pleasant voice answered.

"Hi. I'm calling about the dressing table."

"Sure. It's a woman's piece of furniture. Been sitting in the corner of my garage since I moved in."

Lanae tried to picture a face with the voice and came up blank. "Can you tell me a little more about it?"

"It's old. Been in the family for some time. It's turned that dark color that old varnish gets over the years. There are paint splotches and rings from cans. Stuff like that. But it's solid."

"It sounds lovely. Do you know how much you want for it?"

"Well, it's genuine oak, I guess handcrafted, and should look real pretty when you're done refinishing. I was kind of thinking seventy-five, but you'd have to take a look."

"Where can I see it?"

"I'm on acreage southeast of Lincoln."

Hmm, a country boy. By nature or transplanted?

"That'll be a breeze to find. I'm in Platteville. When would be a good time?"

"I'll want my chores out of the way. Would midmorning tomorrow work for you?"

"Sure thing. How about directions?"

Lanae grabbed a pen and wrote down landmarks and turns before ending the call.

With a sigh, she turned her attention back to the smell of baking cheesecakes, which was now curling up the stairs. She had slipped downstairs to make sure the shop was locked up tight. She lived in the loft over the store now that Moselle and Eric would live in his home.

She had never even baked a cheesecake for her husband while he lived. Was there a man to replace

Keith in her future?

Though tired, the joy of adventure burbled through her as she later prepared for bed.

"Thank You, Lord. Tomorrow I plan to do something more exciting than loop yarn around a crochet hook. Please give me a safe and enjoyable drive through the countryside. Open my eyes to all You have for me to see, to enjoy, to live, to bring glory to You.

"I'm alive. Thank You again, Lord." Lanae snuggled under the covers, and added with a yawn, "And for the ability to look forward to tomorrow."

The prayer calmed her heart, but anticipation filled her mind.

She'd be in the country again.

The guy's phone voice intrigued her. She kicked herself for not asking his name. Could he be single?

She chuckled at herself as she rolled over to get more comfortable. Ah well, it was in God's hands.

The old oak piece would undoubtedly fit right in with the shop's décor as a display nook, maybe even a cranny for their goods. She wondered what kinds of stories the antique vanity could tell.

2

Wherever I am, I aim to be in the here and now.

For most of the thirty-minute drive, Lanae had the window at half-mast. The air was crisp with the clarity of fall. Inevitably, winter's chill loomed as a shadow just around the next bend of the road. She breathed in the freshness, more invigorating than the cool side of a pillow on a muggy summer night.

She matched the rural street names according to the man's directions. When she turned onto the gravel road, she slammed on the brakes.

A handful of wild turkey hens leisurely strolled across the road in single file.

She slowed to the shoulder. With a hand flat against her crashing heart, she commanded her body to relax just as fast as it had accelerated. Her heart slowed back to its normal beat.

As she watched the processional, her phone rang. The wild turkeys took the jarring noise in stride as though they heard musical jangles every day.

"Hello?"

"Hi, Lanae," Geneva responded, "just wanted to let you know Moselle called to say she and Eric are having a wonderful time."

"I sure didn't call Mom on my honeymoon."

"Neither did I, but Moselle and I have always

stayed in touch. Have you arrived yet?"

"About there."

"I'm anxious to see that furniture. Bye now."

Lanae flipped her phone shut and searched both ditches for a tom or drake. Neither adult nor younger male of the species could be spied, so she pulled back onto the gravel road. Turkeys didn't have four legs, but they could damage a vehicle—not that she wanted to hurt them either.

She drove on, beyond the tree-trunk chainsaw carvings of two large eagles, one sitting atop a nest. Her stomach fluttered with anticipation, excitement, adventure. She had no idea of the cause.

Homesickness clawed its way into her throat when she turned onto the rock drive. She belonged in a place like this, where tires crunched over gravel. Lanae brushed away a tear at the sight of a horse silhouetted on a hilltop in the bright morning sunlight.

"Calm me down, please, Lord. I don't know what's going on within my restless soul," she whispered.

Through all the wasted hours of her illness, she hadn't allowed herself to think of the ranch she left in the western part of the state. Except for last night, she'd concentrated her idle thoughts on the creation of *Frivolities* with Geneva.

And she sure hadn't had the energy to yearn for the outdoors while fighting her disease.

She rolled the window all the way down to breathe in the cool country air. Catching the smell of hay and horses on the breeze, her gaze roved the land. Small rocks rolled and resettled beneath her tires as she crept to a stop.

The sky was clear and enormous where it met the

horizon. The whinny of horses carried up from a pasture on the other side of the barn. The acreage represented everything she loved about being outside the city limits. Expanse, horses, a sprinkling of trees in the distance...God's country.

When she caught sight of the cowboy, the vision was complete.

She sighed. Home. How crazy. She felt like she'd come home.

The cowboy rounded the corner of the wood-sided barn that she guessed to be sixty feet long. He loped in the loose way of a man comfortable on the back of a horse.

And she enjoyed every step as he approached.

He even tipped the brim of his hat. "Mornin'. You Lanae?"

Wow was the only thing she could think to say. But she kept it to herself.

Her mouth went dry.

His nose was bent, just off to the right of center. He had a full bottom lip, thinner upper, all accented by what she supposed was a year-round tan. Myriad facial lines gave testimony to a life lived outdoors. She cleared her throat in order to answer. "That I am."

"Sage Diamond."

When he drew close enough, Lanae was dumbfounded at the impact of his eyes. They were an unbelievable piercing blue with a hint of lavender.

"Did you have any trouble finding the place?" Sage spoke in an unhurried manner.

Lanae wondered if he felt rushed about anything. She started to open the door.

"You always leave your car running?" A hint of amusement tugged at his mouth.

Oops. She turned the key. *Great first impression.*

He held the door.

Still caught in the lavender blue of his eyes, shadowed now from his hat, Lanae swallowed what felt like the chaff of an August hayfield.

No more singles ads for me.

His unflinching look was as direct as hers. Lanae's whole body reacted with a whisper of sensation. The surprising zing of attraction crawled over her skin from head to toe.

"No trouble finding me then?" He tilted his head a tad to one side.

"Oh, your directions were exact. It's a perfect day for such a lovely drive. And the wild turkeys topped it off."

"The turkeys can be a treat or a nuisance, depending on how you look at them. Hope you find the antique to be better.. It's in dire need of fixing up. Down in the garage side of the barn. We have to walk a piece."

"No problem."

She followed him over tufts of dormant short prairie grass. They walked toward the barn, a hundred yards away. She paused a moment while he rolled open the over-sized sliding door. Lanae stretched her unused calf muscles. She hadn't walked much since she'd been sick.

Entering the barn, Lanae felt as though she stepped into her past. She paused on the threshold to soak in poignant reminders of life spent on the ranch with her husband. She ran her eyes over the layout of the barn.

She inhaled. Hay, dust, horses, leather.

She listened. The rustles and thuds of cats, horses,

wind.

She took it all in. The surroundings welcomed her.

She longed for home. On the ranch.

I belong in a place just like this. Why tease me now, Lord?

What had she given up?

Lanae shook her head to clear her muzzy thoughts, and looked around.

The barn had two regular sized stalls and one narrower, complete with matching hitching posts for possible troublesome equines that deserved special attention. An overhead door marked an area probably used as a garage.

Lanae didn't know if she wanted to spend time exploring the barn and the creatures that inhabited it or the antique she had come to buy for *Frivolities*.

"Something wrong?"

His smooth voice wrapped around her, making her feel secure.

She met his gaze with a smile. "Not at all. It's all so familiar. I left a life like this when I moved to Platteville, and this feels so comfortable." *Like I've slipped into my favorite old chenille robe, which I really need to toss one of these days.*

Sage made a sound that was somewhere between a chuckle and a groan mixed in with patience. He shot her a questioning look but asked nothing. "Dresser's this way."

The first sight of the vanity drew a delightful, "Ahh," from Lanae. "It's perfect."

In burl oak, the center drawer was swell-fronted and double handkerchief drawers bookended each side. Straight back legs and curved front legs added character.

"It's high enough for a chair to fit underneath." He slanted a grin in her direction. "For a little gal like you."

Her smile was spontaneous. His compliment thrilled her.

She drooled over the delicate piece of furniture. She ran a hand over the curved shape of the largest drawer and pulled on the glass knob. It slid right out, bringing with it combined scents of vintage perfume and faded dusting powder, familiar fragrances from her childhood.

Construction was solid, pegged with dowels rather than nail or screw, where the drawer sat on a full-sized support board rather than slats. A decorative piece of wood rested at the base of the vanity top with mirror supports behind. Too bad the mirror wasn't attached.

She plopped down in the straw, paying no heed to what she might get on the seat of her faded denim jeans, and leaned underneath the vanity to have a look.

A flash from childhood hit her as memories sometimes do. She and Geneva used to crawl under their grandmother's round oak table in her roomy kitchen. When they were really small they crouched on the legs that supported the pedestal. One time the temptation was too much to resist, and using the fork she'd held, Lanae carved her initials in the bottom of the table leaf. Naturally, Geneva followed suit.

"Anything interesting down there?" Sage's voice brought her back to the present.

"You're right. It's solid and well crafted." Lanae was a little disappointed that she hadn't found initials or some other personal markings. She slid out from underneath, took his offered hand, and stood to dust herself off. She stepped behind and found the unfinished streaks in the wood, scarred from screw holes meant for the mirror supports. "Do you have the mirror?"

"Sorry. Haven't run across it."

"The vanity's not much without the mirror, but I still see enough charm that I want it for our shop."

"Since I can tell you'll take good care of it, I'll lop off twenty-five."

She offered her hand. "Deal."

Lanae experienced a jolt when their hands joined. It was as though she'd had a triple shot of Geneva's flavored espresso.

Sage slid his gaze away and let go of her hand. Fast.

She searched for something to say. "Um, it won't fit in my trunk, will it?"

He chuckled, low and loose. "Platteville, you said? Got it covered. I'll be checking on a saddle up north of Highway 34."

"Oh, the lady with the horse-themed strip mall, the western shops? I keep meaning to stop in and check out the competition."

"Lorinda Watts. Doesn't sound to me like your businesses are of the same kind. Since the saddle maker is a short jaunt south of Platteville, I can sure bring the dresser on up in my truck."

She located a dark blue pickup truck, looking huge parked next to the ranch house. And she took her first look at the home. Circa 1970s, the house wore its faded cedar siding as a badge of honor.

"The fireplace inside must be humongous judging by the size of the stone chimney dominating the north side."

She pictured wood everywhere inside, letting herself imagine a home similar to the one she had shared with Keith, the love of her youth.

"It's pretty much the same as when I first saw it when the vet lived here. Haven't changed much at all."

Lanae got the impression that if interrupted, Sage would not repeat or lose his train of thought, but continue speaking at a steady pace. That mannerism matched the language of a man who listened to horses.

And she imagined she could listen to such soothing talk for quite a spell. "Then I'll add in some gas money."

"No, ma'am. Twenty extra miles is nothing if you're used to driving in the country."

Men and their trucks.

"My husband would have said the same thing."

"Would have?"

Lanae stopped and gathered her thoughts. She gazed off to the east, at the hill to the right, and then scanned trees to the left where she imagined a creek flowed. She had no doubt Sage and his acreage might fulfill what was missing in her life. *Impossible to know that so soon.* From the south, a huge V of geese came into view.

She caught Sage watching her. They shared a smile over the thrill nature brought.

"My husband was killed in a ranching accident." She blew a sigh, felt his eyes on her, and looked off into the sky again. "I'd like to have their vantage point."

She felt his steady gaze remain on her while he answered. "I often raise my eyes to the sky, feeling the same way. In summer, a great blue heron glides over the land. Saw a pair back in July."

"No way. I've never seen a pair of herons," she

said, in awe. "I saw one appear once in a while in the distance when I lived in the Sandhills. They're so huge and graceful, prehistoric looking. I wondered what they thought of me on the ground."

Sage shook his head and grinned. "Like minds and all that. I've wondered the same thing, but most of the time I'm no higher than the back of a horse."

"How I miss seeing the land from horseback. I was always so relaxed when I was in the saddle. Yet sometimes it was hard to contain the sense of anticipation. You never know what's on the trail around the bend."

3

The next day, Sage kept thinking about Lanae Petersen and her comment about the trail around the bend. She was a western gal all right. Why the devil did she keep coming back to his mind? It irked him, having the woman there at the edge of his thoughts.

Well, the devil could keep those tempting thoughts.

Or God, for that matter, Whom he was still mad at for taking Becca from this life while in the prime of her life.

"Oh, God, will I miss her the rest of my days?" Sage raised his eyes to the cloudless sky. "Why, why didn't You take my life, too, when You stole my love from me?"

His ragged voice sounded wounded to his own ears. No use talking to the heavens. He'd done enough of such wasted talk over the years.

God had yet to answer.

Sure bet he'd lived with his horses too long.

As long as I don't answer my own questions, I guess I'm still sane.

But the picture of Ms. Lanae Petersen, petite and fit, with short salt-and-pepper hair, wouldn't leave him in peace.

Lanae had chosen her steps with care when she took off toward the barn, as though her muscles were sluggish. Yet she had an underlying familiarity with the roll of dirt beneath her feet. He should have asked where she used to live. Her reference to a ranch in western Nebraska made him wonder about her past. He pictured her in her denim jacket and skinny jeans. She'd even worn boots that were none too new. She had nicely defined legs, just like a good filly.

She had downright shined in the sunlight. The sparkles and lace on her jacket over some kind of riotous-colored shirt had brought brightness and life to his day.

Sage gave Freckles, a paint horse with only a sprinkle of white blotches across the rump, a curious look. "You can tell I'm in some kind of fine mood, can't you?"

The mare didn't answer.

Sage was comfortable with silence.

Silence is where he liked to live.

Or did he? His mind sure hadn't been silent with Lanae and her colors bouncing in and out of his head.

Truck parked at the barn—the woman had even commented on his wheeled beast—he loaded up the dresser. After padding the corners, he tied down the furniture piece with bungee cords, then jumped in and headed north.

The drive to the farrier's shop took him longer than it should have because he pulled off twice to answer his cell phone. He made arrangements for a new horse to be boarded come spring. And he took a call from his daughter, Lezlie. They talked about a good day for Jaxson to visit.

"Suppose my grandson's grown another inch."

"At least two," Lezlie said with a laugh. "Love you. Gotta go, Dad. Bye."

He shook his head over the fast-paced life his daughter led as a working single mother.

To keep Lanae out of his head, Sage mentally ran through his list for loading up the two pack horses for the western hunting trips. Placement of the packing gear on the horses—saddles, saddlebags, hobbles, and canteens—had to be arranged just so. He wanted to go over hitches and knots and the whole procedure the next time Jax came to the acreage.

Sage planned to use the opportunity to explain to his grandson how to get hold of the reins and practice backing up, working the horses onto the ramp and into an open trailer. He'd remind Jaxson to use simple commands like soft throat noises along with his knees.

Bet Ms. Lanae Petersen looks right at home on the back of a horse.

He shook thoughts of her off once again. Since guide horses mostly walk over rugged, rocky terrain, Sage pictured the route. He would lead Jax over a dirt road that was currently under construction. The knowledge his grandson gained riding now would come in handy when he took the boy on a guided pronghorn-sheep hunt as a graduation gift a couple years down the road.

The horse details and mind pictures of Lanae kept his thoughts occupied until he arrived at the row of western-themed businesses south of Platteville. Then he remembered how Lanae had reacted when he mentioned coming here and considered introducing the entrepreneurial women.

Lezlie had teased him a while back by calling Lorinda his lady friend. That's what she was. A lady. And a friend, but that's all.

Lorinda Watts had done a fine job with her shops,

aptly titled Western Row, where variations of whatever a country guy or gal needed were most likely available. Local artists with a knack for leather works, jewelry, paintings, bronze, even wood chainsaw sculptures, now had a fine outlet.

When he pulled up, a kid was swinging around one of a handful of iron hitching posts outside the building. The child's long, straight brown hair flew a beat behind. Sage couldn't tell if it was a boy or a girl.

He strolled past the boots store where a bright display featured a mannequin couple arrayed in Western wear. The scene tempted a guy to step right in and buy.

For some reason, he pictured Lanae Petersen as the all-decked-out faceless female. No doubt, she even line danced.

So much for keeping her out of my head.

He entered the saddle shop, pulling in the smell of leather oils, new and old. He bypassed the old horseshoes in the farrier area and avoided the antique anvil on display. The smithy tool reminded him of his Grandpa Earl. He never wanted to be reminded of the old coot.

Sage went right to where Lorinda attended to tooling a design into Sage's saddle.

"How's business?" he asked in greeting.

"Just fine. Thanks to you, I've got a couple more saddle orders. But if a horse needs shoed in the midst, I'll handle it." She nodded toward the horseshoes and tools in question.

"Saddle's looking good. How long?"

"You'll have it by Christmas as promised." Her wide smile and nod assured him.

Sage tipped his hat and left.

When he stepped back into the sunshine, reminders of the way Lanae had sparkled greeted him anew. An unwelcome curl of some long-ago-buried emotion crawled low in his belly. Sage wanted only two women to be in his thoughts. His dead wife and his daughter.

Get out of my head, woman!

A short time later, he turned off the highway and onto Platteville's Main Street. He could have found *Frivolities* without the name scrawled across the window. The front door and display windows were so decked out in pine boughs and Christmas bows and some lacy ribbon stuff that he burst out laughing. No competition for Western Row at all. The stores were planets apart.

No way was he walking through that fancy door on Main Street.

Sage stepped on the gas and circled the block. He entered the alley and parked behind the store. The back entrance to the place was every bit as decorated as the front. *And then some.*

Greenery wound up the stair railing, around the landing and top deck. Fake poinsettias curved above the sliding door and off a second-story deck where lights twinkled in the shadow of the roof. Warmth and light invited a woman to knock and enter.

He wanted to run.

Who would have dreamt a place off an alley in downtown Platteville, Nebraska, could look so inviting. To women with shopping in their blood.

And scary to men.

Was Lanae Petersen a high-maintenance woman? He doubted it, the way she seemed so at home on the acreage.

27

Lowering his eyes to ground level, though, he wanted to jump right out and explore the mini courtyard off the back entrance. Complete with curved path, he took in the bench, small table, fountain, and handsome windmill created from stained glass. He would have done it different, added some rocks instead of colored mulch.

He accepted the unspoken invitation to move closer and was halfway to the door under the stairs when Lanae stepped through.

"I thought I heard a diesel rumble back here."

"That you did, ma'am." He didn't want to feel so good at the sight of her.

"Sage, I do appreciate your manners. But please, you can use my name."

He nodded but didn't acquiesce.

"Let's get to it." Lanae strode past him and went to the nearest side of the truck bed. She propped a foot on the running board and stretched on her toes to unhook the bungee. Her energy and agility made a lie of her petite, feminine appearance.

Sage let the tailgate down and climbed inside the bed of the truck while she undid the remaining cord.

He let the cords drop and slid the vanity along the piece of supporting plywood. He had the antique against his chest before either of them spoke again.

Lanae scuttled around the front of the truck and under the stairs, where she held the backdoor open wide.

Mindful of the garden furnishings, he followed her inside. She pointed to a long counter just inside the door. Refinishing supplies—cans, brushes, rags, and tools—were lined up and waiting for the dresser.

Lanae brushed a hand down the side of her fancy

apron. "We in *Frivolities* boast the town's best flavored coffees. Want to come in for a cup?"

"Thanks, Ms. Petersen, I drink it black." He backed out the door. "I'd like to take a closer look at this stained glass windmill outside."

"Rainn Harris is the artist. He's in love with my sister."

Sage didn't have an artistic bone in his body, except for his rock garden. He admired the stained glass work and hoped to meet the artist.

When Lanae returned with the coffee, Sage drank fast and thought it was a shame. The aromatic brew called for lingering over. "The day's a-wasting. I best be on my way."

"Thank you again for delivering the vanity."

"Don't know if it'll ever happen, but I'll give you a holler if I run across the mirror."

****

I will include Jesus on this life journey.

Years before, Lanae had tried to refinish a buffet. She wound up making a huge mess of the oak veneered top, and had to turn it over to a professional.

"Thank you, Sage's mother, or whomever. This vanity is solid oak. No veneer in sight. I am thrilled."

She was also glad she started the project here in the back storage area rather than up in the loft, where the smell would have drifted down and scared away *Frivolities* customers. In the storeroom, she could crack the alley door open for ventilation.

Brushing on the solvent to loosen the old varnish on the top of the vanity, the active chemicals made her think of Sage. Rather, her reaction to Sage. The two times she'd seen him, somnolent feelings had started to bubble to the surface just underneath her skin.

The memory brought a smile of pleasure. She'd told her sister about her first sight of him. "You've always been a sucker for a guy in a cowboy hat," Geneva had responded.

For sure, after meeting Sage, all desire to delve into the singles ads disappeared. She'd tossed her stash of newspapers right in the recycle bin when she returned from his acreage.

She slid on plastic gloves, smoothing the fingers. She pulled the handkerchief drawers out and stacked them next to the center drawer. One slot wasn't as deep as the other.

"How odd is that?"

She looked underneath the vanity to check for mismatched support boards. Nope. One solid board, as she remembered from before. She fumbled for a flashlight and looked in the corners of the deep slots where the drawers fit. A piece of wood kept the short drawer from going all the way back. She slid her hand inside. The thin wood rolled up.

Lanae jerked in surprise at the touch of a different texture inside the opening.

Using the light again instead of her fingers, she leaned in close and spied a packet of folded papers and heavier writing sheets wrapped in faded red ribbon. Letters? The thrill of discovery made her tremble.

She imagined the letter writer spritzing the essence of perfume, autographing the air as well as the paper the scent Lanae first noticed when Sage showed her the vanity.

Did Sage know about this hidden space? Hadn't

he mentioned the vanity had been in his family a long time?

"I'd venture to guess he doesn't know about this secret compartment, or he would have kept the contents," she said, tapping the letters against the vanity top.

She set the flashlight aside and held the letters in both hands. The temptation was too much. She slipped off the faded red ribbon and smoothed out the top sheet.

"He definitely would have kept the letters, if..." She looked down at the rolling cursive script on the uppermost letter.

"I wonder if this Katherine, or even Ted, is a member of Sage's family," Lanae mumbled with a shake of her head. Did all women of a certain age talk to themselves? She couldn't tell herself to get a life. She had one, thanks to *Frivolities*.

She unfolded the stack of letters, smoothing the creases. Then she fanned the sheets of paper to note the dates: 1959-1960. They were in order, earliest on the top, most recent on the bottom.

Lanae licked her lips. Her heart fluttered with curious uncertainty as she separated the top letter and laid it on the counter.

Monday
December 28, 1959

My Dear Ted,
I was so glad to hear from you. I was afraid maybe you weren't around anymore, that you had followed your temper and took off.
But why, Ted, don't you write more? I am so anxious to

know whether you are working or not, and what you've been doing all this time. Please write all about it, won't you? Last time I heard from you, you were working in the granary for your dad but wanted to go off and build city streets.

Is your mother working on your grandpa's farm?

As for me, I've been doing about the same old thing, day after day. I help in the bakery until about ten or later when the early rush is done then I come out here to the country for the rest of the day.

Sometimes I feel married, cleaning the Forsell bachelors' home. I imagine it's your shirts I'm ironing.

I am thinking of going to Omaha in the spring and trying to get a better job. I don't know if I will or not. I have several girlfriends working there now, and they didn't seem to have much trouble finding work. I've had plenty of bookkeeping experience here at the bakery. I've been practicing on the typewriter, so I should be able to hold a good job if I ever got it. Our business has been pretty good. With so many women working in the new factory, they are baking less at home.

Did you get lots of Christmas presents, Ted? I fared pretty well, I think. I got two boxes of handkerchiefs, some perfume, bath salts, and powder, stockings, and a nice linen tablecloth from my girlfriend in Wyoming. Evidently she thinks I'm going to be married. She better guess again, unless a certain man I know takes the hint.

Say, by the way, Ted, I had my picture taken at Christmas, and it's pretty good. I might consider sending you one if you'll send me one of you. I've changed a little since you last saw me. I think I weighed about 132 or more then and only weigh 117 now. Fifteen pounds is quite a bit of weight to lose. The baked goods were getting to me. I think I look better thinner, though, and I feel better.

Do you think you'll make it up to Platteville—

Lanae shrieked. "Platteville? This letter was written right here in town?" She continued to read:

...again soon? I long to see you, and to know you are well.
Write to me, dear, real soon, won't you?
Love,
Katherine

Lanae turned over the floral stationery, noting again the date the letter was written.

"Who are you, Katherine of Platteville? Who are you, Mr. Ted with no last name?" The thrill of a mystery tickled Lanae's stomach. "Well, Katherine, whoever you are, I imagine you're a couple generations older than me."

Would Sage have any idea who Ted and Katherine could be? She grabbed the cordless handset and punched in his number. He answered immediately.

"Sage, Lanae here. I've discovered the strangest thing. It's so exciting. And mysterious."

Lanae pictured Sage shooting her a smile of indulgence.

"There's a hidden compartment in one of the handkerchief drawers. I found letters."

"Excuse me?"

"Letters. In the vanity. Do you know anyone named Ted? Or Katherine?" She wondered if they were still connected. The silence was so heavy. "Sage?"

"Got another call."

4

Had he really been so rude as to hang up on her?

Her call had, without a doubt, taken him by surprise. No way was Sage going to tell Lanae Petersen the Ted in question was his mother's brother, his favorite uncle.

The uncle who disappeared one Fourth of July when Sage was just a little tyke and whose name hadn't been spoken since the nineteen seventies.

And for good reason.

But Sage hadn't known it at the time.

His mother sat at that dresser in her bedroom often. She must have found the letters after Ted disappeared. Now, what was this connection with his uncle? Who would have written to him?

He shook his head, confused, and somewhat dazed. "Don't go there. The past is best kept in the past."

And Lanae Petersen had no business sticking her nose in his family's darkness. Her call had prompted him to go right out to the barn. He'd searched until he finally found the misplaced mirror. Once he took it to Ms. Lanae Petersen, she'd be out of his life. He used the callback feature to reconnect with the twenty-first century.

Lanae answered on the second ring.

"Sorry about earlier. I found the mirror this

morning."

"Oh, wonderful. Did you remember where you'd stored it?"

"Ran into a friend who helped me move in. I never knew where they stuck it. The mirror's in the rafters above the tack corner of the barn. Tucked away so it wouldn't get broken, I reckon. We must have gotten busy when we unloaded, so no one told me where it was put for safe keeping."

"I'll come get it. And bring the letters."

"You don't have to—"

"But I want to. Please? I'd really like to meet the horses. And could you show me around? If you have the time, that is."

He couldn't help the laugh that jolted through him. Her liveliness was contagious. Sage felt like a giant smiley face had just rolled over him, keeping the ugly secret of his past at bay.

"Nope, I don't mind introducing you. Since you're getting such a bargain on the dresser, you can bring me a thermos of your sister's great coffee."

"I can do that. And I'll bring some black cherry cheesecake to boot."

They agreed on a time and disconnected.

In the barn, he positioned the ladder where he'd need it once she came for the mirror.

Then Sage tended his horses, whistling while he worked. He fed and watered, curried and combed, and stroked. The four horses kept him good company.

A door slammed outside the barn.

"Yoo-hoo. Coffee and cheesecake at your service. Yoo-hoo, keeper of the acreage."

The smile was involuntary. He didn't want Lanae Petersen to sound so good. She looked even better. He swept his gaze over her when she stepped through the door. There wasn't much wrong with her.

She wore those skinny jeans again, and some kind of wrap that looked like it came from the back of his Grandma Juanita's davenport.

Sage waved a hand in greeting and turned to the utility sink. "Let me get the horse washed off."

While he dried his hands, she poured coffee from a thermos and stuck a cup of savory, strong caffeine under his nose.

He inhaled the heavenly smell of coffee beans. It lifted his senses. "What is it?"

"Some exotic name with java on the end, which only my sister could tell you. Geneva does all kinds of fancy tricks with coffees and flavored syrups."

He thanked her with a nod. Once his hands were free of the towel, the taste delivered everything he expected. "Let's take this over to the bench in my rock garden, shall we?"

Sage led Lanae through the back of the barn and down a small hill to his rock garden. He looked around, trying to view it from the eyes of someone else. Created to accent flowers he'd dug from a friend's ranch pasture in the Nebraska Sandhills, he felt the satisfaction of a job well done.

"This is spectacular!"

For some reason, her reaction pleased him.

"I would love to see it in June. Tell me about the flowers. We had so many on the ranch. Where did you get all the rocks?"

They sat on an iron bench warmed by the sun. When he took the plastic container Lanae handed him, their shoulders touched. He whiffed the scent he associated with her—a little vanilla mixed with spice, and—what else, varnish? He had no business pondering the way she smelled. He leaned into the corner of the bench. Better, and safer, to answer her question. "Not much to tell. Spiderwort. The main plants are long gone, but the sun brings out tiny sprigs of new growth. Those dried up ones are beardtongue."

"The ones with those bell shapes?"

"Right. Some old guys call 'em bluebells." He shrugged and blew before sipping and savoring the coffee.

"That's what we called them on the ranch."

"They're both prairie-type flowers my mom said always reminded her of me." *As well as her brother Ted.* Sage balanced the thermos between his knees, lifted a corner of the plastic container, and handed the lid to Lanae. "Thanks. This is quite a treat for a bachelor." He took a bite. Approval formed in the back of his throat. "Mmmmm…I can't decide if I like the coffee or the cheesecake better, but I think I'm in taste heaven."

Lanae played with the plastic lid in her lap, a contented smile softening her features. Their arms brushed, and somehow the air around the bench became smaller, filled with this exuberant woman.

Bad idea, having her here like this, sitting so close.

He shoveled in the three remaining cherries that slid off the top of the slice and gulped the last of the coffee. He would have liked to swipe his finger through the plastic square to get all the crumbs but good manners were too well ingrained.

When he stood, he set the cup and container on the bench. He turned to wave an arm over the garden. "These granite rocks are all over this part of Lancaster County. Farmers don't like 'em cause they mess up machinery, so these are compliments of the neighbors."

"Most men wouldn't like them. They're pink."

Sage shrugged and let it go. The rocks had provided a project to pass the time.

Lanae put the lid on the plastic container and stuffed it and the thermos in her shoulder bag. The bag was a riot of color that she seemed to like, judging by the way her fingers stroked the zipper closed. She leaned her tote in the bench corner, sighed as though she'd rather stay seated, and rose to her feet.

He could watch her graceful movements for a month.

Then she turned and picked her way along the stone path. She bent to study a huge rock with shells and other fossils imbedded in the surface. He stopped a good three strides behind.

"Isn't God great, the way he gives us pleasure through nature?" She turned and stepped toward him, squinting up into the sun so the fine lines fanned around her hazel eyes.

"You haven't said anything about family except mentioning your mother and grandmother, Sage. Have you lived here long? Do you share this lovely land with anyone besides your horses, or do you live here all alone?"

Something about the way she looked at him, so open and expressive, made him swallow. An uncomfortable tightness grabbed him inside, twisting a latent need to connect with a good-lookin' woman.

"Been here five years." His chest rose and fell. He moved his gaze away from Lanae. "I had a wife."

He felt, rather than saw, her lean forward. She looked as though her whole body tilted to receive more of his words.

"She's dead." Too abrupt, but easier to say that

way. He shot her another glance as she straightened.

Her hand touched her chin, one finger brushing her bottom lip. "Oh, so did my husband. As I mentioned, an accident on the ranch."

"Ovarian cancer."

"I'm so sorry. That's such a horrible disease. What was her name?"

"Rebecca."

He might just as well fill her in, she'd keep asking. Sage had guessed enough about Lanae Petersen to figure she'd only be satisfied with details and having everything out in the open. Too bad he kept so much to himself.

"Becca was a Nebraska girl. A typical one. Sporty, sassy. She worked hard and played hard. You remind me of her. You seem to be a what-you-see-is-what-you-get, sort of all-American type. Becca put the word heart in heartland." He groped for words that lodged in his throat. "She was so full of life..."

"You still miss her."

Sage didn't comment on the obvious.

"I'll never go through that again. That helpless feeling of watching her be so sick. And I couldn't do a blasted thing to help her." He clenched his jaw, felt the muscle jump at his temple. "I'd never go through something like that again. I couldn't stand to watch another person die." *And I'll love her for the rest of my life.* Sage hardened his reaction to the shock, the compassion he saw on Lanae's face. "To answer your original question, Becca never lived here. My daughter Lezlie came and went a couple times."

"Well, it's hard to put it there, but even the Bible tells us not to live in the past. I was sixteen forever ago. Keith was older than my parents liked, but I had written to him when I was in junior high, while he was fighting a war that never made any sense to me. He stayed enlisted after 'Nam and was home on leave at Christmas when he asked me to marry him. I didn't blink an eye. I loved him heart and soul. Quit school in tenth grade and finished my GED later."

"'Nam got over right before I was old enough for the draft."

"You must be a little younger than I am, in your early fifties?"

"I'm with you, same generation. Becca and I got married the week after we graduated from high school. It was a wild time to grow up, wasn't it?"

Lanae giggled that joyful school-girl sound that clutched him somewhere deep inside. "Wild is a good word for it. Crazy bell-bottoms, wild music, from soul to The Beatles."

Sage burst out laughing and turned away. "What I remember is all that feminist talk."

"I don't know if it was feminist or not, but I'm sure glad when it came about that men could help women take care of the home."

They sobered. Sage stared at nothing far off in the distance. "People think we're in troubled times now. Even though I was a little bugger, my folks were shell-shocked for years over the King and Kennedy assassinations."

"Mine as well. Patriotism and all. Keith pictured Jesus instead of Uncle Sam pointing His finger and saying 'I want you. So unclutter your mind and let me in.' He obeyed Uncle Sam and Jesus. He believed that being a little bit saved is like being a little bit pregnant. Either you are or you aren't."

Sage couldn't find humor in the pregnancy

reference.

He formed a fist and started to pace. No way would he comment on her reference to Christianity either. But he faced her, after putting a good-sized rock between them.

"You miss him, too." He said, repeating her words.

"I do. At times." Lanae zigzagged to the outside of the rock garden and started walking. "Especially here in the open. We were so at home, so in love on the ranch. We had it all."

They matched strides in silence, headed in the direction of the barn.

"Tell me about your daughter."

"Lezlie is a nurse in Lincoln. I'm so glad she turned out as well as she did."

Lanae brought up God. So I will do so as well.

"For a long time she carried a good mad-on at God."

The way I will forever. He clenched his fists. What was it about this woman that drew him to talk? "Lezlie was fifteen when Becca died. Thought God had betrayed her by taking her mother, so she went out and slept with the first boy to give her the opportunity." He bent, picked up a twig, and twirled it in his fingers. "Jaxson was the result. He's the apple of my eye."

Lanae stopped and squeezed his arm right above the elbow. The feminine touch of her fingers shot through him.

"You have a grandson! We were never blessed with kids." Lanae became intent, stared off into the distance as he had earlier. "I had some issues that resulted in surgery that kept me from ever having children." Her hand drifted from his arm to wave in the air at her side.

Sage had no idea what to say to that. She must keep nothing secret. He went on with his own train of thought. "I'm not going to say the road has been easy. But it's worthwhile. Family is worth more than anything. And we need to protect the ones we love."

"No doubt about it. Moselle, my niece, and Geneva's daughter, is the next best thing to a daughter an aunt could wish for. She always thought I was hard on her, that I somehow expected too much. But we talked it out not too long ago and she understands how I only wanted the best for her. And she's found it now that she's Mrs. Eric Todd."

They stopped at the corral fence. Sage rested his elbows on the top rail.

Lanae stepped onto the bottom.

Their elbows touched. Neither one moved.

"Keith was killed by a skid steer loader. Out in a pasture doing who knows what. It's hard to imagine him now, in his sixties, about the age my dad was when he died of a sudden heart attack."

"Don't I know it," Sage agreed. "Accidents happen to farmers and ranchers. People in the country gotta be thinking about what they're doing all the time."

"That you do. As much as I miss the land, I don't miss the stress. Who'd want to be a rancher these days? You live with unreliable weather, unpredictable cattle prices, critter deaths. West Nile." Lanae's voice rose with each issue. "A growing mountain lion problem. I'm glad to be in a small town, now."

They watched the horses nuzzle aside leaves, looking for remnants of green grass on the other side of the far gate.

"What are their names?" Lanae asked.

"Freckles, the paint, and Snorty next to her, are mine."

"Quarter horses have heart."

"Yes, ma'am, they sure do. Spooky and Ranger belong to a guy who only uses them for hunting. They were pretty wild when I first met them."

At the sound of Sage's voice, all four horses moseyed up to the fence, each trying to get closest to his hands. He couldn't help but chuckle as he brushed their noses.

"How long does it take you to get a horse to do your bidding?"

Sage pushed the brim of his hat up with a finger and resettled it. He'd rather talk about the horses than his work with them. "Less than a day."

"That's an incredible gift."

"It's just something I do."

"So this hunting, it's in Montana?"

"You got it. Bighorn mountain sheep in the early fall." It tickled Sage that she appeared so interested.

"And you're able to get the horses used to commands and being packed and ridden again in such a short time? It could take Keith days to settle a horse. You must be a horse whisperer, a man who meets the horses on a spiritual level."

"You do know horses. I get 'em ready early in the summer, then just ride them and enjoy them until the owner comes for the trip west. This year the guy decided he likes the way I take care of his horses, so they're boarded here for now. And will stay here as long as it works out."

He made the mistake of looking her full in the face. And such was the impact of her green-gold-brown eyes, Sage felt as though he'd been kicked by

Ranger. She licked her lips, and he wondered what she was thinking before she spoke.

"So, tell me, I'm curious to a fault. How did you get such an unusual name?"

Sage swallowed. He was close enough to pick up her scent again, so strange here in the outdoors. And oh boy, did she smell better than a horse. He couldn't name it, but he believed he'd recognize Lanae's scent in a crowd, female and fresh, hers alone.

He tore his gaze back to the horses. With so much oxygen in the great outdoors, why did he feel like he couldn't get a deep breath?

Sage tried to remember Becca's dark brown eyes. Then he decided to talk, instead. "My mother said my grandmother Juanita named Mom and my aunts after purple flowers: Iris and Lilac. Violet was my mother. When she took a look at me she thought of the prairie spiderwort flower. Then she said out loud to my folks, 'purple sage.'"

"Well, I love it."

"No way was my mother going to call me anything purple," Sage continued without humor, "so she settled for Sage. I guess Mom agreed with the name. Gramma used to say that Uncle—" *I almost said Uncle Ted's name!* Sage pretended to cough. "Uh, she said my uncle's eyes were the color of wild blue flax." He stepped back from the fence. "Enough about family." *Anything to get off that subject.* "Tell me about this business of yours," he invited.

Her eyes lit up. Her whole face turned animated. He couldn't help but laugh when she started to speak.

"Oh, it's just so crazy, and I love everything about it! Perfect for the three of us. Moselle knows antiques and can drop some old designer names, but Geneva and me? We wouldn't know a furniture designer name if it was engraved on a thousand-dollar handbag. But we do like old things, especially if they're handmade." She mimicked using a crochet hook. "We believe in handcrafted items with our names, though. Geneva quilts. I crochet. Moselle does creative artsy stuff with a glue gun. She came up with the idea for *Frivolities* shadow boxes."

"I can sure tell what you're into. What else?"

"Merchandise women like, whether they're three or eighty-three. Lots of fancy and silly, frilly stuff. We cater to females. Young and old alike. Some older gals come in and buy a small porcelain doll or a reproduction of something that reminds them of their childhood. We sell vintage things, too, like ruffled aprons and handkerchiefs. And right after Christmas we're going to start etiquette classes. Playing dress-up with young girls, and the whole afternoon tea time with delicate sandwiches and flowered teapots."

"Well then. Whatever you say. You make me want to catch my breath." He threw his head back and laughed.

She had as much energy as a galloping steed.

"Let's fetch that mirror."

Anything so she forgets the name Ted.

Yeah, right. The way I've forgotten what he did.

****

There is so much more to life than a beating heart. I want to be more and feel more than just hanging around for the next breath.

Lanae noticed every movement Sage made as he picked up and repositioned the ladder. She watched and enjoyed the play of muscles in his forearms, thighs, back. So many thoughts chased through her mind. After the comment Sage made about illness, she couldn't tell him about the disease that nearly killed her, hepatitis C. Like many, he wouldn't believe she was cured.

Here in the barn, all her senses had come to life. Lanae tried to take deep breaths. She even counted and stopped at her age, fifty-three. Keith was the last man she had reacted to with such tingling awareness. The memory felt like a lifetime ago.

I am a woman.

Sage is all man.

Moselle and Geneva found their mates.

Could mine be in front of me, Lord?

Her gaze followed Sage as he climbed the ladder. From the rafters, she picked out a glint of the mirror caught in the sun's reflection through the open door. She looked closer. The frame was made of swirled pieces, the glass itself oval, hinged at each side so it tilted. Her fingers itched to touch the old frame.

"Oh, I can't wait to get it all refinished and put together. We plan to display the vanity as a backdrop for some sort of Christmas decorations," she said when he brought the mirror to the top of the ladder. Lanae stepped to the ladder and lifted a hand to help balance the mirror so Sage could descend less encumbered.

"Thanks. Looks like the glass needs re-silvered or replaced, depending on your choice."

"Re-silvered. Then again, maybe left original is the best. The edges are beveled, so I may want to keep it as-is."

He bent over so they could set the mirror down, Sage taking most of the weight before he climbed the rest of the way off the ladder.

She was so close to his shoulder that all she had to do was move a half inch and she could kiss him. Her lips parted, she drew in air and blew it out as quietly as she could.

The smells of the barn, the dryness of the hay, mixed with the distinct, moist smell of horse leavings, took her right back to the ranch where she and Keith had shared so much love.

But this isn't Keith. This is Sage Diamond. And he's as sweet smelling as his name.

She inhaled his own unique blend of manliness, the slight tang of sweat, and the hint of horses on his jacket. He smelled every bit as good, as mouthwatering, as a silvery leaf of sage growing in a pasture or garden. She had often savored the spicy condiment at the peak of its summer growth on the ranch.

Sage Diamond.

Suspended in the moment, Lanae couldn't move. Couldn't draw a breath. She closed her eyes. Her lips felt swollen. Her uneven mouth breathing seemed to emanate from the pit of her stomach. She absorbed his body temperature, so much higher than her own.

Sage thrust his shoulders back and brushed her nose.

She couldn't control the urge.

Lanae puckered and kissed his shoulder, the well-worn fabric of his denim work jacket tickling her lips.

Time stopped.

Does he feel me?

Horse nickering and shuffling faded. All she could

hear was the pounding of her heart.

Or was it his heart?

The air vibrated with tension.

They were alone in this world, his world.

Feeling alive after serious illness was one thing. Sure, her mind and heart sought joy and fullness of life. But being around Sage felt like she'd been transported to the forever ago. Back when she was sixteen, coming to life in the presence of the love of her life. She felt as awake as a new bride, quickening in the height of awareness, as though she were in love. Lanae jerked back. And almost tripped over the mirror.

Love?

Lust?

Lord, what's going on here? Should I be feeling this way?

She mumbled something, too embarrassed over her behavior to articulate any thoughts. It had to be the acreage. The man drew her as much as the land did.

Sage finally turned, brushing against her shoulder, and grabbed the mirror frame at the same time. He hoisted the mirror, his movements uncharacteristically jerky. Then he released the mirror in the air before grabbing it on each side, which prevented the mirror from swiveling in its frame while he carried it toward her car.

Lanae unlatched the trunk and stood by her driver's door. Sage loaded the mirror.

She was all shook up. And she didn't even smile at the picture of Elvis that flashed in her mind with her choice of words.

The passion she had imagined when she read the love letter seemed like a single grain of oats in a feed bucket compared to the flood of sensation she felt at the base of the ladder.

Sage slammed the trunk lid and came to her side. "Guess that's that, then."

She must have looked like an idiot standing there, tongue-tied, lips parted, but nothing coming out.

He was tall enough, broad enough, to block the sun. Sage leaned, pursed, and smacked a feather-light kiss in front of Lanae's ear.

"Better than a handshake, huh?" His voice held a joking, teasing quality. But he didn't meet her eyes.

Geneva's favorite words flitted through her head. Twitterpated. Discombobulated. Flummoxed. Now she knew how flustered her sister had felt at the resurgence of all those reawakened teen hormones, which was Geneva's response to Rainn's attention.

And my response to Sage. Good golly, Miss Molly.

Forget all the age stuff.

Besides, what's age got to do with love?

God's love is based on eternity. Age means nothing to Him.

But age and widowhood had made her fail as a rancher. The only way she'd make it working the land again would be with a man by her side. She shook her head to get rid of ridiculous longings. How she got in, turned the key, put her car in gear, and backed up, she had no idea whatsoever.

Forgotten in the excitement of finding the mirror, and her awareness of Sage, the old packet of letters remained on the passenger seat. She glanced at the bundle, inclined to head back up the driveway, but she decided to leave them for the time being. She put the transmission in Drive and hit the road.

****

Halfway home, turning from one highway to the next, Lanae pulled over, too shaken to continue driving.

As sudden as a deer can leap out of the ditch into a car's path, the past slammed into Lanae.

She'd been this tuned-in to a man one other time in her life.

And her husband hadn't been the man.

Recollection of the affair, a part of her past that was buried so deep it took over twenty years to resurface, jostled to the forefront of her mind.

Her loneliness for Keith had been palpable, and she'd tired of the despair. So she'd let a stranger in. She refused to dredge up the details of that dark corner of her past. A Christian took Christ along when delving into sin. Lanae grieved anew over grieving the Holy Spirit. Now she cried a year's worth of unspent tears as the history of events wove through her mind.

Giving up the ranch. Leaving Keith buried in western Nebraska. Elation over a new life with Geneva and Moselle in Platteville. The beginning of *Frivolities*.

Dealing with the onset of fatigue and a potential terminal illness. The shock, the uncertainty of the diagnosis.

She knew there'd been talk. People in small towns meant well, but they talked about everyone's business except their own. Dirty needles, drugs, and illicit sex—that's what gossip came back to the shop.

What seemed like a week, but had only been minutes, drew to a close. Lanae gathered herself together. Not one vehicle had even passed. She stared off into the distance, focusing on nothing. Eventually, she blinked and settled her sight on the passenger seat.

Lanae picked up the bundle of letters, played with the ribbon, smoothing the creases where it had faded.

Love was timeless. Just look at how happy Geneva and Rainn were. She and Geneva had been messing around in *Frivolities*, spoofing about how much the media focused on the young and beautiful and pretty.

"I think God shows humor as we age." Geneva said. "Life and death are His idea. So aging must be as well. We learn a lot on this journey called life. Choices, wisdom, changes in attitude. He looks at the inside as he prepares us to grow into the people He wants us to be."

That process took a lifetime. The Lord had a purpose in bringing people together, no matter their age. Lanae thanked Him for Moselle and Eric, Geneva and Rainn, and the glimpse into the love Katherine had for her Teddy.

Lanae had copied the letters, intending to give the originals to Sage. "So I'm curious. I'm a romantic at heart, interested in a love from long ago." She laughed as she talked out loud to herself. "I am going to read the letters one by one," she said to a flock of blackbirds. "So shoot me."

She imagined Katherine's words as her own, reaching out to Sage, rather than addressed to Katherine's Teddy.

She set the top letter aside, and pulled out the second. Lanae figured she'd miss the faint scent that unfolded with this original letter of longing. The copies she'd made would just smell like paper, stuffed in a corner next to her chair in the loft.

As she read, it felt as though Sage were right beside her, along with the mysterious Katherine and her Teddy. She read the letter out loud.

January 15, 1960
Friday a.m.

Dear Teddy,
It's funny how for all the letters I write, I never get an answer. Hint, hint.

Thank you for the movie. You were so restless though. I don't think you were truthful when you said you were all right. I could tell you were in pain. Did you fall in the grain bin and were too embarrassed, or proud, to tell me? I couldn't determine if it was your ribs or back, but I knew something was wrong.

I wish I was there to kiss your pain away.

Honey, I have so much work to do today. Why don't you come help me? Do you suppose we could get along working together? I can't quite see you in a bakery, though. Or us keeping company for long hours when you close up and keep things to yourself.

Well, sweet, the time is flying, and I never know what to write about, only you. I do think about you all the time but need to sign off now and get to work.

Here's a bushel of xoxoxoxoxoxoxoxoxoxoxos and lots of love,
Katherine

Katherine's concern wrapped Lanae in a blanket of empathy.

She felt the love.

She remembered the agony of separation after Keith died. But God had pulled her through. After a time, she'd started living again. And she wanted to keep living until her own dying day. Curiosity burned. Was Ted hurt? What had made him angry?

She thought of Sage and wondered again if he had sensed her hormonal overload at the bottom of the ladder in his barn. The way she had kissed his shoulder through his clothes.

And then her distinct pleasure—like something palpable hanging in the air.

Was he as thrilled by her closeness to him as she was whenever he came near?

Could he feel her desire?

Her yearning for Sage, like Katherine's for Ted, was growing almost too large to shape into words. It felt like a consuming fire. She tried to imagine some kind of invisible concentric waves, like a translucent aura, radiating off her body. The vibes she envisioned were for Sage alone. And she planned to be tenacious as she went after him with all her might.

Whether Sage liked it or not, Lanae was attracted to him, as much as to his home in the country. And the secret surrounding the letters, of course.

"Face it. You want the whole package."

But a little voice whispered, *is this of the Lord, or a personal desire?*

Lord, help me put it behind me. I'm so sorry for my sin. Forgive me for yearning toward Sage. My future is in Your hands. Now I just ask that you keep me safe as I return home. And, thank You that Sage found the mirror.

5

Sage couldn't get the woman off his mind. And oh, how he wanted to get Lanae Petersen off his mind. Didn't he?

Those hazel eyes, ever changing in prominent color, had kept him from a good night's sleep.

He left his bathroom and went into the vaulted great room of the ranch home. Sage blew out pent-up lungs full of air as he surveyed the room. "You were so fine, my love."

Becca didn't answer. Her frozen smile beamed into the expanse from where it perched on the mantel shelf. Sage didn't check the tears that gathered as he crossed the floor. "You'd be so proud of Lezlie. And Jax. He looks just like her. Tall, red-haired, scads of freckles. Except he has your eyes. And he wears a size fifteen shoe. Can you imagine?" He ran a crooked thumb over her smiling lips. The glass felt cold.

Lanae had been all about heat. So full of life that it hurt him to watch her. She'd warmed the air around them.

He gripped the edge of the rough-sawn pine plank of the mantel shelf, locking his elbow.

And just that fast, his tears dried. His breathing hitched.

He had felt feverish with Lanae Petersen in the barn as her warmth reached out to him at the base of the ladder. Sage doubted he could have moved if lightning had struck the peaked roof. He'd heard the expression of time standing still but until that moment had never experienced it.

He had sensed her awareness of him in her placidness, almost like she was breathing him in. She was so close that he had imagined her embracing him from behind. And it had taken a mountain of willpower not to turn and grab her close.

It'd been so long since he'd felt that way.

Not since Becca was alive. *But Becca hadn't made my pores sweat inward.*

Their desire, his and Lanae's, he reluctantly admonished, had been thick in the air. It was a felt thing, an almost tangible longing he couldn't put a word to. More than a physical level. Those reawakened feelings had come out of nowhere.

Lanae Petersen had come out of nowhere.

All because he decided to get rid of the dresser.

She'd answered an ad in the paper.

He'd taken a phone call, given directions.

And Lanae Petersen drove directly into his life.

He hadn't moved back there in the barn. The experience was a spiritual moment, when her soul reached out and touched his on a plane he'd never known existed. The moment had shattered when Lanae mentioned Christmas.

Christmas always reminded him of Becca. How could he forget the holiday that turned his world colorless? Becca had died on Christmas Eve. And the life he'd known became history. Every year since then, he'd taken Lezlie and Jaxson on a trip instead of celebrating Christmas.

And this year, he planned to look at some

property while they were on vacation in the sunny South. Nebraska winters were getting a bit too harsh for his constitution. It was time for change.

But, what if a new life experience was right here at home?

****

If it's worth going through, I want the experience now.

"He's tied to the mystery letters. I can feel it in my soul." Lanae spoke to a gold and white display of angel ornaments as she went about the business of *Frivolities*, preoccupied with thoughts of Sage.

The letters stayed on her mind, and turned into her excuse to stay in contact with him. The letters belonged to him. Or, someone in his family.

She couldn't get the writer off her mind. Katherine—whoever she was—had emoted such passion through her words. Lanae read between the lines and imagined Katherine as stirred up over her Teddy, much as Lanae remained shook up over the barn episode with Sage. What had possessed her to behave that way?

Throughout the day, the cowboy came to the forefront of her mind except when she was talking shop or busy with a customer.

Lanae glanced toward the front when the jangling bell announced another potential buyer coming through the door. Smile of greeting in place, her heart picked up its pace.

The sight of Sage sauntering into *Frivolities* drew a grin. This cowboy was way out of his element. He removed the hat, revealing his close cut brown hair and a serious what-have-I-gotten-myself-into frown.

Lanae, as well as Geneva and Moselle, wanted all men to feel out of their element in *Frivolities*.

Only this guy made her breath hitch, and her spine stiffen to full walk-with-a-book-on-your-head attention.

Hmm, maybe the women should do something about that. Create a masculine corner? She tucked away the nugget and planned a men's shopping guide as an idea to bring up with the others.

For now, her every cell felt riveted on the man shutting the door behind him with complete mastery, like he didn't want to make a whisper of a sound as the latch clicked back in place.

Too late. The bell had announced his arrival.

He looked down at his hat as though he'd never seen it before and arranged it back on his head at the precise angle he wanted. Then Sage rolled on in, gaze ever on the move. His muscles bunched, clearly defined in upper body and legs. That V-shape of a cowboy—complete with hat, boots, turquoise belt buckle, and narrow hips fitted into snug denims.

Lanae's mouth went dry. Sweat prickled her palms.

Something twinkled. Was that really a diamond stud in his ear?

She felt as though every nerve ending in her body woke up.

When he was close enough for Lanae to catch the scent of the outdoors on his clothes, she looked down at his working man's hands. They were white-scarred and rough, with knobby, swollen knuckles that reminded her of Geneva's arthritic fingers.

And then she swallowed, trying to digest the idea

of his hands touching her. The calluses would be rough, yet she knew those hands calmed horses on a daily basis.

"Hi. I washed these for you. We left them on the bench in my rock garden." His voice drew her gaze to meet his.

"Thanks. Sage, you didn't have to bring them in. I haven't even missed them yet." Lanae hadn't noticed that he carried her thermos and plastic container

"That's OK. Talked to Lezlie this morning about the day Jaxson is going to spend with me and I realized that it's almost Christmas. I haven't got a thing for her." He swallowed and looked around, frown lines deepening.

His grin gave Lanae a glimpse of the little boy he must have been.

"I figured this would be a good place to get something different for her." His gaze roved and came back to her face. "Lezlie has enough western things. Besides, that theme really isn't her thing anymore."

"Where would you like to start?"

"I'm kind of afraid to move around much in here. So. Haven't a clue." He shot her a sheepish grin. "You sure do have a lot of woman-stuff."

"That's the whole idea." She couldn't help but answer his grin with a wide smile of her own.

He was so out of his league.

She loved it.

"Can you tell me a little about Lezlie? The colors she likes, or does she collect anything?"

His eyes appeared to refocus. "Turtles. She loves turtles."

"OK then. As wild as it sounds, it just so happens Geneva has a wall quilt with a turtle motif."

She led him through displays of Victorian tree decorations, cat and dog themed items, linens in a refinished pie cupboard, feather boas, tiaras, and other little girl things that turned them into princesses.

"Who does the fancy work? Doilies, aren't they called? My mom used to do stuff like that. It's nice and feminine, if you like that kind of thing."

Lanae sighed with pleasure. Sage noticed the fruit of her hands. So warmed inside by his compliment, she felt her smile spread. "Yes, they're crocheted doilies. Those are some of my contributions to *Frivolities*."

He fingered the three-dimensional flower on a table runner, his broad, tanned hand looking so masculine against her finery. His rough touch gentled probably so he wouldn't snag the linen where it met the crocheted rose.

"You do good work." He returned his hand to his side. "Where are those turtles?"

Lanae got a kick out of watching expressions on the faces of customers. She'd remember this customer's reaction for quite some time.

When she showed him the wall quilt, his frown turned into a smile. As though a weight had lifted, he murmured, "It's perfect."

Lanae was proud as punch at Sage's reaction to Geneva's quilted piece.

"Orange is Lezlie's favorite color. She likes olive green, too. But it reminds me of the military, so I don't quite get how any woman can like it." He tilted his head and returned his attention to the appliquéd quilt. "I would have never thought to put orange and purple together."

"Geneva can't help herself. Purple is her favorite color." The last two words came in stereo.

Sage raised a brow and tipped his hat to Geneva.

"Welcome to *Frivolities*. And I'm going to guess that your name is Sage."

"That it is, ma'am."

Geneva extended her hand, catching Lanae's eye in the movement. "So, who else likes the color purple?"

"My daughter likes orange. And she has a thing for turtles so I don't even need to ask a price. This artwork is sold."

"Sphtt," Geneva sputtered and splayed her hand at the base of her throat. "Artwork, indeed. It's just what I do."

"The way Sage listens to horses," Lanae said.

"I understand you have a wonderful home." Geneva continued as if she'd not heard her sister's comment. "Lanae wants to move back to the country now, thanks to you."

"I never said—" Lanae began.

But Sage jumped in, "Well, I wouldn't know about that." He avoided a direct look at Lanae and spoke to the hanging turtle. "Think you could wrap that up so I can be on my way?"

"I'll rustle you up some brew for the journey. Caramel flavored coffee with white chocolate syrup sound all right?"

Sage joined Lanae's laugh at the wording of Geneva's offer.

Yup. Lanae could get mighty used to cowboy lingo again.

6

A guy could sure get used to having women like Lanae and her sister around. Geneva's coffee was a fine thing. She had refused payment. Lanae had gift wrapped the quilt for Lezlie at no charge. Just because they didn't celebrate Christmas, didn't mean he was stingy with gifts. Sage raised his eyes to the ceiling of his ranch-style house where narrow slats of darkened pine slanted to the center beam.

Those sisters were something.

He surveyed the great room as he hadn't done in a long while. Would Lanae like the inside of his home? Most ranch homebuilders used a lot of wood paneling in their construction. He examined the over-sized dark brown leather and heavy wood furnishings. His gaze skimmed over the wrapped package for Lezlie. He imagined Lanae's crocheted scarves and dainty lacy-looking things dotting the tabletops.

What would Lezlie think of Lanae?

No time to ponder that now. A door slammed outside, announcing Lezlie had arrived with Jax.

Sage moseyed outside to greet them. Lezlie felt thinner when he hugged her. Jaxson had more muscle to his shoulders and was taller as well.

Lezlie didn't stay long enough to let the motor of her fancy SUV cool before she blew him a kiss and rolled back down the driveway.

Sage looked forward to the days he spent with Jaxson. Since Jax turned twelve, those days came less often. These kids had way too many activities to keep up with anymore. Guess if they were busy, they kept out of trouble.

He threw an arm over his grandson's shoulders. "What do you plan to do with your time now that football season is over?"

"Mom wants me to check out some volunteer stuff at the hospital, but I'm not sure that's my thing. I'd rather come out here."

"You'll have your driver's license before you know it, Jax. Help me finish feeding the horses and we'll go inside. We should find some good football games on TV."

Jaxson pointed at the horse standing in the corral. "You sure calmed that paint down, Grandpa. I remember how freaked out it acted first time I saw her here."

They stood at the fence, gazing at the horse in question, just hanging out.

"Like I told you when I first brought her home, the horse had been mistreated."

Jaxson shot a confused look at Sage. The boy was so tall now that their eyes were level. "I don't understand that. How can a guy be mean to a horse?"

"I grew up in a time when it was OK to beat an animal. It was even common to beat a child or a wife."

"Don't get it."

Sage waited a beat before he commented. "Me neither. What makes you angry, Jax?"

"I dunno. Never thought about it. I just get mad, sometimes." Jaxson frowned in concentration, freckles merging. "Things I can't do anything about, I guess."

"You're old enough to hear this. Maybe your mom has already talked to you about it. A prime example of anger that drives you to do unexplainable things is the way your mom acted after your grandma died. Lezlie hopped into bed with your father. It was a deliberate act. She reacted out of anger." Anger at God, but he didn't add that qualifier.

"That's heavy-duty action, I know. But it's OK. We've talked about it."

"Where does that anger, that violence, come from except a deep-seated need for control when life throws you a curve?"

"Mom would say anger comes from hatred. And hatred comes from anger. And lies. So...Satan, I guess."

"Your mom's pretty smart, Jax. I'm not going to say she hated anybody at the time. But I'm sure she hated a life that she felt had blitzed beyond her control."

"She doesn't talk much about Grandma. But she has told me she was mad at God, and her behavior was wrong." Jaxson's Adam's apple bopped with his swallows. "Why do some people need anger to gain control, Grandpa?"

Sage let the silence stretch as he contemplated the hard emotional lesson Jaxson was grappling with. He should be enjoying his grandson's company amidst the serene horses instead of the crisp air becoming thick with their heavy topic.

But some memories were too thick to block out all the way.

Sage had grown up hearing his mom tell about the ever-present rage her father, his Grandpa Earl, had harbored through her growing-up years. He yelled and cursed at Grandma and his aunts and mother. Yet never laid a hand on 'em.

But Grandpa Earl let loose and unleashed his anger toward Uncle Ted. Sage understood from his mother that his grandfather had beaten Uncle Ted with anything handy—belt, board, black razor strop.

Yet Sage remembered his uncle as being patient and kind. Uncle Ted never once told Sage about being beaten, demonstrating that age-old tradition of keeping ugliness hidden in the closet.

Jaxson eventually remarked on the topic but with a sneer in his voice. "Seems like anger goes far in earning respect, too."

"No reason for sarcasm here, Jax. It's all about clear expectations. I can read a person's, or a horse's, body movements. But I lay no claim to being a mind reader."

"Sorry, sir."

"It's OK. I just want you to remember that people make a horse crazy. No horse I've ever known was born crazy."

"Kinda like people, huh?"

"I'd say you're learning today, son."

"Grandpa, I think I'd like to learn how to train a horse."

"Let's plan on that for next summer then. We'll talk to your mom and figure it out. "Sage ruffled Jaxson's carroty hair. "First things first, Jax. If you learn nothing more from me, get this. I'm not a trainer. I'm a listener, maybe even a gentler. But I don't train horses. Horses and I work at communicating with one another. It's all in body movement and how man reads a critter."

"And critters read men." Jaxson smoothed his hair onto his forehead, separating and stretching hunks past his brows. "Yes, sir."

"I got your mom's Christmas present today. Let's go in for some hot cocoa and talk about our trip this year."

"Awright!"

Sage ruffled Jaxson's hair again for the satisfaction of the boy's reaction. Oh, to savor life with a teenager's verve.

Or with sassy Lanae Petersen's outlook.

7

Savor the moment. Don't endure it.

Ten minutes after Sage exited with his gift for Lezlie, newlyweds Moselle and Eric Todd bounced through the front door.

"Well, don't you look all tanned and happy?" Lanae greeted them.

Her niece and new nephew-in-law gave her a hug from each side. As she stepped back, Moselle asked, "Where's Mom?"

"I think Rainn just dropped off Mia, so they're out back saying good-bye."

"We're here now. Hi, guys." Geneva rushed in for the requisite hugs. "You've lost weight."

Moselle and Eric exchanged silent communication. Moselle presented the picture of a blushing bride, red hair and green eyes so like her mother's as a young woman. Lanae had to remind herself of the year.

"Would you believe I went jogging on the beach with Eric?"

"What kind of honeymoon escapade is that, for crying out loud?" Geneva waved her graceful hand in the air.

Lanae joined the fray. "Can't imagine running on the beach for exercise. A beach is for serenity. To me, a sports bra is like a girdle for the ribcage."

Eric rolled his eyes. The women laughed because they got the reference.

After more laughs and hugs for Mia, who waited her turn by rubbing her wrists across her hip bones, Eric jostled Moselle close against his side. He planted a rousing kiss on his bride. Then he waved himself out the door.

Lanae sighed inside, imagined such a moment shared with Sage, and had a hard time tuning back in.

Moselle announced, "The beaches and the turquoise waters of the Caribbean were great. But home is where my heart is. *Frivolities* memory boxes await."

"Now, honey. Your heart needs to be anywhere Eric is."

Mia accidentally bumped into Geneva, trapping her hand against the counter. She grimaced in pain.

"I thought you were on a new arthritis med, sis."

Geneva tossed away Lanae's concern with a smile then nodded to the customer entering through the front door.

During the lull in traffic flow following the lunch hour, Lanae latched on to her idea of shopping guidelines for men. She approached Moselle and Geneva where they were cleaning up the coffee counter. No way was she going to wait for their Monday business meeting.

"What do you two think of a shopping guide, or suggestion sheet or brochure, a manual of sorts, for men seeking gift items here in *Frivolities*?"

Moselle stared off as though she was trying to decipher handwriting on a wall.

"I'll never forget the way Eric reacted when he saw all those pictures of you, Moselle," Geneva responded first.

"He told me later he had to wade through the froufrou to get to me. And then I was more than he could handle."

"You still are," Lanae and Geneva chorused.

Lanae shot a glance toward the referred corner where painted green vines crawled up the wall, surrounding an antique armoire. Fancy-framed pictures of Moselle rested on shelving gussied up by Lanae's doilies in varied sizes and designs.

"And Rainn. If he hadn't tasted your coffee, Mom, I doubt he would have come through the door."

"Let's think about their reactions, and comments of other men who have ventured in, and jot down ideas. Use your card drawing talents, Moselle, see what you come up with for marketing." Lanae had to raise her voice on the last four words because Moselle got busy at the espresso machine, swooshing and whirring to make her favored frothy latte.

"How does a shopping list compare with greeting cards?" Moselle yelled.

"I just cleaned that up!" Geneva gave her daughter a jab with her elbow.

"Haven't had my latte yet today. I'm a big enough girl to clean up after myself."

"Girls, girls," Lanae teased.

The bell above the entry door gave its tinkle and the three looked up. A striking, tall redhead walked through. She strode toward them in a no-nonsense manner and stuck out her hand, eyes never leaving Lanae's.

"From Dad's description, I'm going to guess you're Lanae. I had a day to myself and didn't know what to do. Dad suggested I check out *Frivolities* in

Platteville. So here I am."

Sage-colored eyes, Lanae noticed right off. The freckles and red hair must have come from her mother.

Lanae swallowed, wondering what else Sage may have said. This had been quite a day.

"Lezlie Diamond. Sage is my dad."

"Welcome to *Frivolities*," Lanae, Geneva, and Moselle trilled in trio.

Laughter broke up any underlying nervousness.

"It's so nice to meet you, Lezlie. Sage told me you and Jaxson are his whole life."

"Besides horses," Lezlie said with a rounding of her expressive lavender-blue eyes. A cloud of something else entered her expression but cleared as though the sun had popped out.

Lanae guessed Lezlie and Moselle to be close to the same age. Sage hadn't said. She couldn't imagine Moselle with a teenaged son.

"Are you interested in seeing anything special? Or would you like some coffee and then an opportunity to browse on your own?"

"I'd love some coffee."

Geneva turned to her chrome and brass coffeemaker, ready for action. "Today's special flavor is hazelnut, but I can give you regular blend with flavor. Or latte or cappuccino. What do you like?"

"I would love anything creamy and rich. The black stuff at the hospital where I work gets old."

Moselle looked as though she had walked into the middle of a play not knowing what had happened on stage before her entrance.

"Honey, this is Sage Diamond's daughter, Lezlie. I'll tell you about Sage later. And Lezlie, this is my sister, Geneva, and her daughter, Moselle." Lanae turned to Mia, who pulled at the bottom of Lanae's apron, seeking attention. "And this little minx is Mia Harris."

Mia didn't look at Lezlie, stating instead, "I'm thirsty, too."

Geneva had balked at the idea of caring for an autistic child when Rainn gained custody of his niece and moved Mia to Platteville. Geneva had come to terms with the idea of looking forward to grandmothering, rather than mothering. But loving Rainn, and then falling in love with the little girl, had changed her mind.

Lanae guided Mia by the shoulders over to the small refrigerator underneath the counter. But her ears tuned in as Lezlie explained for Moselle's benefit.

"My dad and Lanae met when he advertised an antique vanity that used to be my grandmother's. Dad told me about *Frivolities*, this chick place that scares him. By the way, I love it!" Lezlie continued. "I dropped my son, Jaxson, off at Dad's acreage. It's the first Saturday he hasn't been with his friends since school started."

"And he didn't want to spend it with you?" Geneva put in with a laugh.

Lezlie smiled her thanks as she accepted the *Frivolities* mug filled with mocha. "Smells heavenly. It's more like I didn't want to spend the day with my son. I've been working some extra hours in Lincoln, where I'm a nurse. Mornings and evenings I get enough of Jaxson's teen testosterone." She sipped, gaze checking out *Frivolities* over the wide rim. "Mmm. This is lovely. Coffee and shop. Tell me about it, please."

"We think of it as a God-thing."

Lanae grinned over how much Moselle sounded

like her elders.

"I'm all ears. Well, and taste buds, right now." Lezlie took another sip of the hot liquid.

"Geneva and I are both widows," Lanae chimed. "I don't know how much your dad told you, but I used to live on a ranch in western Nebraska. Geneva and I saw the ad for this building, and ta dah: *Frivolities*."

"I'll say it again. I love it. I could hide myself here just checking everything out."

"That's what we like to hear. Moselle moved from Kansas City where she used to work in an antique store and for a card company. She has a degree in art and uses her talent to create new items from old things. She's found her niche here now with a paint brush and other tools. Moselle returned to Platteville after I got seriously ill. That's a story for another day." Lanae picked up a fancy shadow box and held it against her chest. "I am so proud of Moselle for using her God-given talents and coming up with the signature *Frivolities* item. We call them Memory Boxes."

She caught the eyes of all women within hearing and continued. "*Frivolities* Memory Boxes reflect the three of us. As you can see, each of us contributes. This one began with a quilted design block from Geneva. North Carolina Lily is the pattern, I think. Moselle, the glue-gun queen, worked in her glued-on beads, buttons, and sequins. Embellishments, you know. You'd be amazed what catches her fancy." Lanae ran a loving hand over the boxed frame. "Then this one is topped off around the edge here with my crocheted rosettes and embroidered trim."

Lezlie took in the ramble with a smile. "Do you mind if I meander on my own? There's so much to see. I'm not looking for anything in particular at the moment. But I'm sure I can find lots of interesting goodies."

"Be our guest." Lanae waved a hand. "Just give me a holler if you need anything from the ceiling."

"You have a lot of inventory, that's for sure," Lezlie said, scanning the merchandise above their heads. She indicated the lathe where a burgundy velvet garland was hanging off-kilter from the ceiling trellis. "And I have to hand it to you for the way it's all over for customers to see." Lezlie took another sip and grinned at Geneva. "This coffee is so good it's dreamy."

Like your dad's eyes and mellow voice.

"Before you look around, and while you enjoy your drink, would you like to see the vanity I just finished?" Lanae invited.

At Lezlie's nod, Lanae led the way to the back storeroom.

"That's our dress-up corner." She pointed to an area where old, and a few new, hats, purses, shawls, beads, gloves, and boas were bunched and hanging from a wall divider.

"I'll bet little girls love that."

"And some grown-up little girls," Lanae added, wondering what Lezlie's mother had been like.

Lezlie paused to study a display of rainbow, butterfly, and dragonfly Christmas ornaments. She made them tinkle with the back of her fingers.

Lanae recognized the little-girl wonder. "Have you ever heard a butterfly?"

Lezlie gave her an out-of-your-gourd look.

"I'm serious. When there's not one hint of breeze and the air is thick with humidity, a butterfly's wings are noisy. I can't count the times I've had one land on me, when I was suspended in time by their tickling touch. Its feelers, sensors, or tentacles, whatever they are called, sipped the moisture from my skin."

Maybe Sage would understand, him being a horse whisperer and all. Lanae tried not to smile at Lezlie's you're-one-crazy-woman look. They walked past the door to the loft stairs and on through the office.

"You must have a connection with butterflies the way my dad does with horses. Lezlie ran a hand over the back of the sofa and said, "Every office should have a couch like this. Better than hospital-plastic, especially with a color the same as my dad's name."

"I've seen that green referred to as celadon, something similar to celery. But I'll call it sage from now on. Your hospital furniture probably helps keep staff awake at night."

"I'm sure you're right about that," Lezlie agreed with a hearty laugh.

Lanae nodded toward the sofa as she held the door open for Lezlie. "The sofa, though, I'll look at differently from now on, thinking of your dad. It's been a comfort, kind of a solace after the hectic attack of *Frivolities* on the eyes and ears."

They shared another laugh. Lanae added, "Not really. The wild colors and goofy stuff just make me smile." Why couldn't she shake her flustered desire to make a perfect impression on Sage's daughter?

The vanity stood alone in the back storage room, shining and giving off a hint of chemical smell.

"As soon as I can't smell the polyurethane anymore, I'm going to set the vanity in the display window out front."

"It's lovely. Is it dry?"

At Lanae's nod, Lezlie set her mug on the

workbench. She trilled her hand over the smooth oak finish. "Dad will be pleased. It looks wonderful. I'm into the chrome and Formica, and white-pine look of about fifty years ago. I just couldn't see this dresser in my home."

"Good for *Frivolities*, then, huh?" With pounding heart, Lanae grew serious. "Did your dad tell you about the letters I found in a hidden drawer?"

"No way."

"Yes, way." Lanae slid the drawer out then slapped the heel of her hand against her forehead. "Would you believe, I drove all the way to his place and the letters are even now on the front seat of my car?"

"Everybody has a lot on their minds." Lezlie picked up the secret drawer and investigated its curious depth. "So, tell me about the letters. Where were they exactly?"

"This is where I met Katherine and Ted." Lanae reached into the hole left by the vacant drawer. "Bend over and watch my fingers."

Lezlie appeared lost in thought for a moment. Frowning, she exchanged the drawer for her mug, tracing the *Frivolities* logo. "Katherine. Ted. I've never heard either of these names. Dad told me about Great-grandma Juanita naming my grandma and great-aunts."

"The purple flower names." Lanae filled in the pause.

"Right. But Katherine and Ted draw a blank."

"Well, as soon as I have some free time, my mission is to discover who they are. The mystery is bugging me at all hours of the day and night."

Along with thoughts of your father.

"Since the vanity was in my family, I'd love to help search. I have Internet service on my phone, so I could do some online searches any time, any place."

"Now, why didn't I think of that?" Lanae raised her gaze to the painted ductwork before leading Lezlie back through the office to the sales floor of *Frivolities*. "I doubt I'll ever get used to how fast technology has changed the world."

Geneva was hanging up the phone. She turned and joined them. "It's an age thing."

Lanae added, "We didn't grow up with this modern techie stuff so we think written tomes rather than keystrokes."

"Like Dick and Jane," the sisters chimed.

"Excuse me?"

"That's the name of the primer we learned to read from," Geneva explained, with an airy wave of her hand.

"Technology may not be what it's all cracked up to be," Lezlie said with a smile. "I think it's pretty sweet, this love letter concept in the day of e-mail, and social media."

Lanae smiled at that. "You just take all the time you want to look around, and remember to ask if you need anything." She indicated one of the display windows. "That's where the vanity will go."

"I'm already drawn to what you ladies have made for yourselves here. Of course, I'll have to check out turtles and other critters. Frogs, maybe, or some other whimsical animals."

"We do have country items. Authentic looking, as well as fantasy. I miss living and working in the country so much I suggested we stock some reminders of the outdoors."

Lezlie squared her arms in the air, elbows at her sides. "This is a no-brainer, if you miss it so much, Lanae. Dad loves to have the horses ridden, and he can't ride four horses every day. I'm inviting you out to ride tomorrow afternoon."

"Sage won't mind?"

"I'll tell Dad when I pick up Jaxson. As for now, I'm shopping." Lezlie put action to her words and began to wander.

Moselle grabbed Lanae's elbow and pulled her into the office. "OK, give me the scoop."

Lanae told her all about the vanity, purposely ignoring the hint to hear about Sage.

"Just think, Aunt Lanae, you could be meeting a bunch of losers from those singles ads. Instead, answering the ad for the vanity introduced you to Sage." Moselle danced a little jig and twirled Lanae around. "I can't wait to meet your guy with the gorgeous eyes. He's bound to be something, judging by what you've just told me. Besides, I like his daughter."

****

"So, Dad, is Ted someone in our family? Who the heck is Katherine? Have you been holding out on me about family history? Are you keeping some grave, dark secret from Jaxson and me?"

Sage felt his cheeks burn with the guilt of omission. Good thing he held on to his summer tan. "Why in the world do you want to go backward? Jax is doing fine in life. He couldn't care less about long gone people from the past."

"Uh, reality check here, Dad. You are stuck in the

past. You stopped moving forward when Mom died. That's half my life. Sooner or later, the mind, body, and spirit will atrophy from all that negative energy you try to hide. Yet, it's evident to me. You need to start living again. Remember, you can't take a horse into your arms for a comforting hug."

Jaxson cracked up, laughing so hard even his ears turned red.

Sage didn't feel like laughing. Lezlie was way too serious when she looked him in the eye. She was on a roll.

"My son and I have taken zeroes for grades in elementary school because you found some excuse not to help with family trees. The most I got out of you was your parents' names. Other than my grandma was Violet and my granddad Myron, I only had Sage and Becca."

She was definitely on a roll. He let her get it out. "Christians aren't supposed to swear, but I swear it's like you are half here. Half-minded, even. And you aren't old enough to have half-heimers yet."

Sage lowered his eyes to his boots and cocked his left ear toward his shoulder. Nothing like being told off by your own kid. His neck cracked when he moved his head to the right.

"By the way, I invited Lanae to come out and ride tomorrow. I know you'll be here."

That brought him front and center. He stared at Lezlie, too stunned to sputter a protest.

Lezlie's words ran through his mind. *You stopped moving forward when Mom died.*

Was it so obvious that he stopped caring about life sixteen years ago? All this time he thought he'd kept to himself how much he missed Becca.

Would he be able to keep the family secret to himself?

"I'm glad Lanae found those letters. I want to find out who wrote them, Dad. If there's a Ted in the family, I want to know. Jaxson needs to know about this side of the family, too. He has no dad, remember?"

****

They can keep their talk to themselves. Gossip is for small minded people.

June 17, 1960
Friday a.m.

Dearest Teddy — xxxx
Thought I'd drop you a few lines and let you know why I couldn't make it last night. Will tell you more when I see you. I was so spitting mad.

But I've seen you that mad. Only difference, I'll tell you why, yet you never have said what gets you so riled up. I can guess. I've heard some talk about your father.

My dad refused to let me leave the house. You'd think that at my age I'd have some freedom. And I work so hard for him. I sweat for the family business.

All I did was drop a tray of freshly frosted doughnuts, ordered by the banker for a special meeting. There were more than enough doughnuts on the shelf. I got them frosted and they were on time, but the way he reacted, a person would think I'd killed someone.

Just one of those things.

This looks like another grand day and me with so much work to do again. I worked from about 3:30 in the morning yesterday, until 3:30 in the afternoon. Then, I went home and fixed supper for my folks. I barely had time to get ready to leave, but my cantankerous father took the car keys.

What kept me going through the night were thoughts of you. I closed my eyes and imagined us together on our special country road. I get all worked up thinking about what your kisses do to me. I'm sorry if that's too forward. But Ted, I want you to take me away from this place so we can be together forever.

Will it really be two long weeks before you are in Platteville again? I would think your father could do without your help more often than that.

But no one works on the Fourth of July.

So, I'll be seeing you then. Be good, sweet, and bye-bye. Lots of love and kisses to you, my dear.

Lovingly yours, and always yours,
Katherine

P.S. How's the neck? I didn't like the look of that bruise. Take good care of yourself. Until I can kiss it for you, Here're xxxxxxxxxxxxxxxxxxxxxx on paper.

Lanae ignored the falling tears, cradled her stomach, where Katherine's yearning had created a churning of her own.

A longing for love.

A desire to be with Sage.

She pictured the young Katherine and Teddy in an antique car, stopped on a country road with a myriad of stars overhead. Would those eyes of Teddy's be visible by moonlight?

Would those eyes of Sage's be visible by

moonlight?

Lanae imagined herself in a car, parked somewhere, sharing kisses with Sage.

The fantasy soon had her choked with longing, and reminded her of how much she had missed over the years. The pull for close contact with a man was almost tangible, entailing much more than the intimacy of physical love. An emotional attachment had resurfaced in her own life, one she hadn't missed until this moment.

No one else would do, Sage was the only one to complete her human loneliness and fill the emptiness. She knew it as surely as there were words printed on the page held in her shaky hands.

Cease, Lanae. And with that word, like a bolt from the Spirit, came the words, *"Cease striving and know that I am God."*

Oh, You are that, Father. And You created me and Sage and emotions. You created soul mates for relationships You ordain. Why am I so restless?

She'd done fine for a lot of years without a man. And even if marriage was God's future plan for her, He'd remain her All-in-All.

She ran a hand over the copy of the letter. The originals remained in a travel caddy in the front seat of her car.

Who are you, Katherine?

And who is your beloved Teddy?

She had to find out. The phone directory would be a good source. Or, she could search town history. The Historical Society had come up with a centennial book in recent years. Maybe something on record would reveal who owned the bakery that closed long before Lanae started high school. Since her mom had been a great cook, the bakery was one store she had never entered as a girl.

And if Sage didn't like what she planned, he could go jump in the Platte River.

Probably wouldn't hurt him to get woken up, to come to life in cold rushing water.

8

I want to get caught in the pouring rain. I want the memory, the feeling, of playing barefoot in oozing mud. Let the rain drip off the bottom of my hair and eyelashes.

At the early service, inside the church entry, Lanae met Rainn. "Good morning, soon-to-be-brother. Mia's off to Sunday school already? I missed saying hello." Lanae gave her future brother-in-law no chance to draw a breath.

He slanted his lopsided grin that accented the lines in his face and went so well with his silver hair. But he kept silent with that indulgent grin.

She looked over his premature gray hair with the curl that Geneva loved and thought for the thousandth time how he was a perfect match for her sister's red-headed liveliness.

"Listen, I've come up with an idea for *Frivolities*, and I need male input. So I'm inviting you and Eric and my new friend, Sage, to a brainstorming session tomorrow in the loft." When she paused for breath, she caught Rainn's chuckle.

"You done yet? What kind of food? Can Mia come?"

"Mia is always welcome. You know that. Moselle's casserole, my cheesecake, your sweetheart's coffee—and Geneva will come up with something else." She didn't give him a chance to accept. "I'll see you then. Now I'll hunt down Eric."

She found him just inside the sanctuary entrance. After their greeting, she jumped in. "Eric, I need your and Rainn's advice on a man's shopping guide. Are you free Monday night?"

"Moselle said something about that idea for *Frivolities*. Will the mystery man Sage be there?"

"I plan to extend a personal invitation."

"Count me in."

The piano prelude began.

"See you then." Lanae lifted a hand and hurried down the aisle to her seat.

****

Lanae got caught up in the music. As much as she had tried to concentrate on the sermon, she forgot the message from the pulpit as soon as she left Faith Bible Church.

Mixed in with her newly awakened feelings for Sage was curiosity over the mystery of who Katherine was. Or is. For the first time since finding the bunch of letters, she wondered if the writer could still be living.

As soon as she returned to the loft above Frivolities, she grabbed a colorful bookmark shaped like a flying dragon and used the straight edge to keep her eyes on each entry of the local phone book. She looked at every first name in every surrounding town until her eyes watered and lost focus.

No Katherine, or the initial K, was listed. She did find Kate Rawlins, the town's infamous gossipmonger. But Lanae couldn't fathom juxtaposing sour Kate with passionate Katherine.

And, who was Ted? Or is.

"He could be alive as well."

Just for kicks, she started all over. The two Teds she ran across, she knew. One Ted was ninety and had a passel of relatives around town. The other Ted was the town mechanic, and he was too young.

Should she come right out and ask Sage if either Katherine or Ted was a relative?

Was Sage hiding something from her?

The phone next to her arm rang and she shrieked. Lanae puffed out her cheeks and blew away her startle before picking up the phone.

"Sage here. Guess my nosy daughter invited you out. Think you can be here after lunch?"

She laughed low, with pleasure. "Good morning Sage. Home from church already?"

"Headed there now. How about being here by one?"

"Sounds too good to be true. I'll be there."

Lanae needed something to fill the hour before she could head over to the acreage. She went downstairs to the office and played around on the Internet. She wished envelopes with names and addresses had been with the packet of letters, but they'd been banded together in one folded loose-leafed package. She decided to leave the task of questioning Sage about family members to Lezlie.

She looked up the meanings for the word sage. She knew about Russian sage planted in gardens, and sagebrush, of course. She had torn off many a sage leaf to put moisture in her mouth while riding on the ranch. The plant was garden or desert variety, member of the mint family with the meaning "to heal."

Was Sage in her life as a healing influence? Or was

she meant to profit from his wisdom?

She also knew that Native Americans used sage in ceremonial smudgings. A glance at the clock ended her search. It was time to leave for the acreage. On the drive to Sage's home, Lanae battled her mixed-up emotions.

Oh, Lord, is it a sin to forget the music or message from this Sunday's worship? Please cover me with the Spirit.

Soon, she turned into Sage's drive. When she stepped out of her car, she closed her eyes. Right there in the driveway, she raised her arms to heaven. She swung and twirled and burst out into song.

God had given her life. His words spoke from between the covers of her Bible. Did she need to remember a sermon?

When her eyes opened, Sage stood close enough to touch, smiling wide, character lines accented, flax-blue eyes snapping. Yummy.

"I'm not sorry," she announced. And couldn't help but smile.

"Didn't say you should be. Good afternoon. And to clear any misperceptions, your exuberance tickles me." Sage kicked up his heels and danced his own little bow-legged hop, grinning like a fool the whole time. "Ready for that ride?"

"And then some. Can't you tell I'm excited to be here?"

The music of the country, the nearness of Sage, opened every sense to her surroundings. Only the tips of nearby trees moved in the gentle breeze, creating a whispered pine symphony. A squirrel's chatter reached her from the road. Soft leaf rustles rose from beneath the hill.

A grating screech shattered the moment.

"Neighbor's truck. I told him he needs to fix those brakes 'cause they sound like a sandpiper on speed."

She couldn't help the giggles that erupted.

Sage gave his little joke a twitch at one corner of his mouth. "I'll take Freckles, and you can mount Snorty."

Lanae looked at Snorty, who was watching her. "It sure is something, isn't it, how horses see in degrees, almost in a complete circle around them."

"Yup. They're only blind right behind the tail. I think he likes your body language."

"Hey there, boy." Lanae stroked his flank then over his withers, down the jawline. He jerked his head up when she untied the reins. She made a soft noise, patted him, and crossed the reins over the saddle horn.

The horse reared his head and took a step back.

"Horses are a flight animal. His instinct is to get away from you."

"I know. But I'm a fight animal, like all humans. He'll get used to me."

Sage cupped his hands to give her a boost up. She settled into the saddle, right at home. She felt the heat from his hand where it rested on the horse, so close to her.

"Snorty sure acted out when I first got him. Had a tender mouth due to chewing on a harsh bit." He shot her a sharp look in the eye. "So, Ms. Horsewoman, have any idea how to get a horse to stop with another means besides pulling?"

"You sit heavier in the seat instead of pulling on the bit in its mouth. You say 'Whoa.'"

"Alrighty then. You know what you're doing. How's the stirrup length?"

"Perfect, thanks. Look at that. The sun is bright

enough that a fly flew out to buzz in the warmth."

"I don't care for pesky insects. One of the things I like about winter is that I don't have to spray." Sage picked up the reins and climbed onto Freckles.

"I'm sure the horses don't miss them, especially deer flies." Lanae clicked her tongue, the "kissing" sound horses responded to, and they loped off.

Sage couldn't pull off the grumpy personality. The sparkle in his eye softened any negative words.

"I once worked on a Texas feedlot. For a bit. But I missed the Nebraska seasons. I don't miss the acre-upon-acre of pipe-fenced pens or the muck and dust that went along with them." Sage gazed off at the horizon. "Those horses, though. Gotta love 'em. They are seasoned with cow sense, work like a calf cutter's dream."

"I can't put into words how much I miss being around horses. I don't miss the uncertainty of ranch life. Each year is a fight with the possibility of a low cattle market, drought, and disease. But living with the big sky, the seasons, nature—I believe is living the way God intended us to."

A cloud shadowed Sage's countenance. "Did He intend for you to lose your husband? For me to lose my wife?"

"Sage, come on. You're a Christian, aren't you? You know God tells us in the Bible that He knows the number of our days. He has a plan for us as individuals. He's in control. Not us."

Clouds hid the sun. They shared a study of the sky. Thunder rumbled in the distance.

"Sure thing we're not in control of the weather." Sage met her gaze and slanted a smile that erased his comment about their joint single status.

"I love the rain," they said together.

"One time I was out on the back deck on the ranch, and I heard what sounded like rain on a tin roof. As soon as I recognized it, the sound moved." Lanae raised her face to the sky. "It rained buckets from south to north. And I listened to the progression as it moved over the roof again."

"Yep. Rain has to stop and start and travel. I'll never forget the time the sun shined in front of the house and rain fell behind the house."

"So a little rain isn't going to scare us away from a good ride, right?"

"Not if it remains a sprinkle," he agreed. "And it's not raining now."

Lanae felt right at home as she learned the rhythm of her mount. She gloried in the warm flesh beneath her and especially in the fact that she was enjoying God's creation with a man at her side.

She pulled Snorty up in order to follow Freckles where the path narrowed along the creek. When the path widened, Sage dropped back. His leg brushed hers while they rode side by side.

"I'll probably tell you every time I'm here..." *Will I be here often*? She pretended to concentrate on where the horse was stepping. "I really do miss the country. Sometimes I mourn outdoor living as much as I mourned losing Keith."

"Country living can have its drawbacks. There are pros and cons to everything in life." Sage gave a silent command for Freckles to halt. "Every time I look at this creek bank I think of how my mother died. She bent down to look at a newborn calf, and the heifer butted her into a tree. Mom rolled twenty feet down a rough bank. She belly crawled and dragged herself back up to the top, through the meadow, under the fence, and onto the road. She was a cut up, filthy mess because of the rainstorm. I've often wondered how much the flashes of lightning helped her find her way to the house in the thunderstorm." He lifted his hat, ran his fingers through his short brown hair, settled the hat in place, and then squinted as he remembered. "Anyway, she dragged herself up the long, dirty rock drive. When she got inside the house, she somehow managed to knock the phone off the wall. Hours later, the neighbor from up the road who checked on her every day, found her and called for help. Of course, it was too late. She was already gone."

"Sounds to me like she went out doing what gave her pleasure in life. Working on the place she loved, doing what she loved to do with her time. Outside, with animals God put in her care."

"That's how I've always thought about it." Sage applied leg pressure and his ride took a step. "And funny thing, I can't help but enjoy a good rainstorm."

The creek bottom widened and darkened as the water gushed in a faster flow and mud swirl.

"I've always had a dream to ride a burro to the bottom of the Grand Canyon." Lanae raised her hands and face to the sky. The cool kiss of the rain heightened her experience. On her sick days, her heart had soared at the thought of living in the moment. Nothing in her imagination compared to the slickness of refreshing raindrops.

"Well, if you aren't careful, you're going to fall into a small cany—"

And just like that, Snorty started up the opposite creek bank. Lanae, surprised at the steep angle, slid off his back. She should have paid attention when the horse started to veer left. She'd failed to let Snorty know she was in control instead of him.

For now, Lanae didn't even try to stay on the horse's back. She freed her boots from the stirrups and went with gravity instead. Laughter burbled up and erupted into giggles, so by the time her seat hit the mud, she plopped her shoulders onto the slick grass and gave no second thought to making a mud angel.

Sage dismounted and reached for her, but his warm handclasp was wet, and he couldn't get a grip. His fingers barely touched hers, yet her whole body kicked into the invigoration of being in the moment, aware of Sage.

"What would you do if I pulled you down with me?"

Rain dripped off the brim of his hat and plopped onto her forehead when he went for a firmer grip.

"I would have spanked Lezlie if she stayed out in the rain like this." Sage said it with a grin that quirked one side of his mouth. Before a full smile formed, his lips straightened. His eyes darkened to more purple than blue.

Her heart kicked into erratic gear. "For real?" A sudden chill took her by surprise. Compared to the heat Sage put off, the difference was extreme. She imagined blood flowing as hot as lava through her system, the sizzle of ice as it evaporated.

He drew her hand to his chest and wiped the mud against the worn denim. Without breaking eye contact, or even looking to see if her hand was clean, Sage drew her wrist close. His warm breath caressed her palm. Then, he kissed one fingertip. The barely-there touch reminded her of fish nibbling her toes in the creek on the ranch.

Lanae swayed toward him.

At the same time, Sage shattered the moment by letting her go. "We're soaked to the bone. It's past time we get back to the buildings."

The skies opened up, and they were, indeed, drenched by the time they walked ten paces to where the horses waited under the protection of a low-hanging cottonwood limb. At least the rain washed most of the mud and debris off their clothes as they returned.

As soon as they dismounted in the barn, Lanae kept her hand on the horse while speaking to Sage. "Thank you for today."

The horse's neck quivered where she ran her hand over the wet velvet muzzle. Snorty's brown eyes looked upon her with trust. Used to her now, he nuzzled the side of her face.

She crooned, continuing the gentle rub down the horse's soft neck. "What a nice, handsome boy you are."

"I'll get the horses dried off. You can't climb in your car looking like that. Go on up to the house. Let yourself in through the garage. Lezlie keeps a pair of sweats in that cupboard by the kitchen door. You can borrow one of my jackets."

"I've got a hoodie in the car that'll work. And thanks again, Sage. Despite the weather, I had a grand time today."

"Guess I'd call the rain and mud a bonus." His smile warmed her from the inside out. She half expected steam to rise off her clothes.

Lanae suspected he was surprised he'd had fun. It had probably been a long time since Sage enjoyed a good time with someone besides his daughter and grandson.

At the house, Lanae resisted the temptation to take a walk-through. She couldn't resist a peek, though. The furniture appeared to be made from pine tree trunks. The neatness and orderliness of the great room came as a surprise.

Her first impression of the house was correct. The inviting stone fireplace took up most of one wall. And made her feel more at home than she knew Sage would want.

****

Visions of Lanae laughing in her muddy, sopping, worn denim floated through his thoughts while Sage attempted to shake moisture off the saddle blanket.

Lanae had looked up at him, all open and willing, inviting him in for a closer view. Her eyelashes had been darkened and spiked by the rain, accenting the stormy hazel shades of her eyes. It had taken a monstrous effort not to pull her close and protect her from a lifetime of thunder and lightning. Guess not. She thrived on the electricity of storms.

The taste of her earthy skin tempted more exploration.

Then a flash of betraying Becca had shot through him.

Maybe he was attracted to Lanae because her clothes were bright and seemed an extension of her personality. A rumbling chuckle built up and escaped. Except today. She was a mess. Still, all womanly curves and hollows, despite her small form.

Then he recalled the touch of her finger against his lips.

"Get out of my head!" He said to the tack shelf where he kept ointments and wraps for horse injuries. The items were all there, right where they belonged, whatever he needed for muscle strain, fibrous tissue, bites or scrapes to sensitive horse skin.

But Lanae stayed in his head.

She didn't belong there, horning in on Becca's spot.

Sage looked for a diversion, tried to concentrate on tack. The snaffle bit he used with a single rein, the bridle, head stall, cinch—all right where they were supposed to be. Too bad he couldn't order his life in neat rows, arranging events as they struck.

Concentrate.

What could he teach Jax the next time he came out? Each horse's mouth has a different level of sensitivity. A shank bit takes a little longer to get used to, but if the mouth is tougher, like a guide horse he'd worked with the year before, the outcome was a good one.

Keep it up. Think horses. Not women.

Rather, one particular woman.

He turned back to equine details and tried to recall the movement of one particular horse, an unruly and bossy guide. But when he got used to Sage, the horse had followed him around like a puppy. He mentally went through the process of flexing the horse in circles from side to side, with the goal of getting the horse to look in toward the rider's knee, while moving in a circular motion. The horse was supposed to stretch its muscles, get all loose and go with the rider.

And just like that, Sage pictured Lanae's hands on Snorty. She wore her nails naked or light pink. And she kept those fingers occupied with crochet hooks.

What would have happened if he'd joined her in the mud?

"No, man. Don't go there!"

But she was already there, in his head.

Lanae was reeling him in, the way she should have reined Snorty the opposite direction before her fall.

Sage even admired the way she enunciated her words instead of sounding like she was chewing or didn't have the energy to finish words without dropping consonants.

"Sage?"

He jumped and whirled. So deep in his head, her approach took him by surprise.

"I was up the road and finally remembered the letters."

He didn't take them from her hand, rather nodded to a small ledge between stalls.

"Well, you're busy..."

He didn't contradict her. Watched her set the letters where he indicated—on a ledge close to her side.

But contradictions writhed in his head.

"Thanks again for a wonderful afternoon."

He offered nothing more.

Her smile faded. She turned away. "See ya."

Sage let her take two steps. "Wait. Look, I'm sorry, but these letters are none of your business."

"O-K..." She mimicked his frown. "But why are you so upset?"

"I plain don't get your pig-headed goal to discover who wrote the letters, and what they might imply." *I've kept the family secret from Lezlie all her life. I'll continue to do so with my grandson.* He wasn't going to give the boy an excuse to be mad at the world by letting him know his great-grandpa had been murdered.

And no one had paid.

Well, that was under dispute. It would do no good to anyone to bring what happened out in the open.

Lanae waved once before she backed through the door. Then she was gone.

He opened his ears to the sounds outside the barn, tuned in to her movements as she departed. After her sedan turned onto the road, and he could hear the engine no longer, he snagged the letter packet.

Without so much as a glance, he tossed the letters into a five-gallon bucket he used for a trash can.

There, his family secret was free from exposure.

9

I know where I'm going, Lord. And I plan to have as much fun as I can until You take me to be with You.

In her favorite recliner for their Monday session, Lanae fumbled with her yarn and crochet hook, and started to count loops. She couldn't remember the last time she dropped a stitch. "It's just no use," she mumbled. "I'm giving up on who wrote the letters. I found no reference, no names for who had owned the bakery years before. There were a couple of old pictures that showed only 'Platteville Bakery' painted on the front window."

"It's pretty weird, all right, that there isn't even a family name recorded," Geneva agreed.

"And it's just killing me. I want to know who Ted is. Every instinct gnaws at me, says Sage is involved somehow. I mean, how many references, in your whole lifetime, have you ever seen to 'eyes the color of blue flax?'"

"None," Geneva said at the same time Lanae answered her own question.

Lanae continued, "Maybe it doesn't matter who Katherine was. Or Ted. I've looked in the telephone directory, entry by entry. Not one Katherine is listed." *Only Kate Rawlins.*

"There's an old picture of Main Street hanging in

the library. The bakery is shown, I'm sure. I'll bet if you asked, they'd take it out of the frame to reveal what's written on the back," Geneva suggested.

"They'll start talking about how the *Frivolities* lady has lost her marbles." Lanae surmised.

"You are really serious about this mystery, aren't you, Aunt Lanae?" Moselle contributed.

"What's a mystery?" Mia piped up. Rainn's niece was keeping the ladies company in the loft.

Geneva explained to Mia in terms her future stepdaughter could understand. Geneva and the other adults in Mia's life found if detailed instructions were given in a methodical manner—and not too many at a time, Mia responded well. Structure helped keep the six-year-old happy and content.

Lanae smiled, recalling the first time Mia got tangled up in *Frivolities* merchandise. She contemplated the little girl. Could autistic children learn to crochet? Maybe later, when Mia was a couple years older.

Geneva interrupted Lanae's wandering mind. "Why are you frowning? You were so hot about ads not so long ago, have you considered putting out a lost and found notice?"

Lanae snorted and tuned back in. "Yeah, right. I can see the bold headline: 'Do you know Ted last-name-unknown?' And underneath: 'I have his letters.'"

"Or how about writing a letter to the editor?" Moselle suggested. "Better yet, let me post something on my social media page."

"Hold on." Lanae raised a hand, palm out. "Anything we do I'd better run by Sage. We're probably talking about someone in his family."

"You're right. But we can still plan. Maybe make a

copy of the undated letter and put it on the counter next to the register? I could use an easel so it's propped upright." Geneva offered.

"Or better yet, in the window? I could help Moselle with a display, spot-lighting the vanity. It's dry by the way," Lanae said as an aside, "and make something on the order of a collage, framing the letter and placing it front and center."

"You go, crochet queen. I love that idea!" Moselle leaned down and gave Lanae's shoulders a jaunty twist.

"Rainn has an antique frame that would be just the right size for the letter," Geneva added.

"And that big old cracked mirror in the storage room we've held onto?" Moselle headed for the kitchenette and tossed over her shoulder, "It's perfect to frame the whole collage for added dimension."

A frame within a frame? Lanae could see it.

Those letters are none of your business. Her subconscious brought Sage's vehement reaction to mind.

"Hey, Lanae, would you read one of the letters again?" Geneva prodded.

Lanae retrieved the missive from her *Frivolities* apron pocket, straightened the folds with the trembling sense she was in the wrong, and read out loud.

My Dearest,

So much between us has never been spoken. I ache to be held in your arms.

I feel the wind against my cheek and imagine your approach. I look at my blue flax in the garden and see your eyes. I answer a cardinal's whistle and wonder what it would be like for you to call me as your soul mate.

I wait and I wait to have an answer. Why have you never responded to my recent letters?

I'll never know why you have not returned to me.

Were your promises of love and devotion only empty words? To what end?

I remain devoted to the memory of our times together. And you remain in my dreams, waking or sleeping.

Lovingly, I wait for you.

Forever,
Your Katherine

Eyes like blue flax? Sage Diamond eyes. This Ted had to be family to Sage. Those eyes weren't a garden variety blue.

Memory of our times together.

Memories of my times with Sage, who said the letters were none of my business.

Two itsy kisses. *One next to my ear, one on a fingertip. My whole world changed.*

Other changes have happened in seconds.

Death.

Life.

Believing and being filled with the Spirit.

I've faced death.

I kept on living.

I have the Spirit.

Now, I have Sage.

Did she have Sage? Lanae believed with all her heart the Lord had brought Sage into her life for a reason.

When she pictured Sage, Lanae said, "Uh-oh."

"What?" Geneva and Moselle questioned.

"Remember, Sage wants me to stay out of their family business. I'd better run this by him before we get more carried away."

"Uncle Rainn's here," Mia announced.

The men arrived all at once, getting acquainted as they shouldered through the door.

Lanae caught the other women's gazes, thinking Mia should call her uncle "Daddy" one of these days. "No doubt about it, we need some men around *Frivolities*."

****

"Hey, guys, welcome. Sage, you've met my sister. Looks like you've met Eric and Rainn. My niece, Moselle here, is still on her honeymoon with Eric. And this big girl is Mia."

How could the warmth of a woman's voice sound so comfortable, reminding him of holes in his life? Sage tipped the brim of his hat toward Moselle then swept it off his head.

"Moselle, Sage is a horse whisperer." The sisters said in tandem.

"I doubt I deserve that accolade. Pleased to meet you, all around."

"Even Lezlie says you have a gift," Lanae emphasized.

He was in trouble if Lezlie had talked about him with Lanae. Especially if they were in cahoots over the letter business.

"I don't believe we're meant to control but to observe and absorb nature. I learn about a horse by watching its ears. I try to see what it's reacting to, ignore it, and let the horse come to me."

"Well, I still say, you're a horse whisperer," Lanae insisted.

"My name is Mia Harris. What is a horse whisperer?"

"I'm pleased to meet you, Mia. I am Sage Diamond. And a horse whisperer is a guy who gets along with horses the way you probably get along with your favorite stuffed animal."

Before he could ask Mia what that animal was, a tap on his forearm drew his attention from the little girl.

Sage took the small notepad Geneva held against his arm.

"Moselle had the idea you could write your ideas down while you men talk about shopping in a woman's place like *Frivolities*. Anything that comes to mind, like what you'd be drawn to, what you'd come in looking for, how we can help. The opposite of what might keep a guy away forever. That kind of thing."

Lanae spoke as she loaded a round serving tray with a mouthwatering assortment of cheesecakes, plates, and forks. "Tell us what you thought the first time you came through the door. What scares you about shopping for women?"

Sometimes the sight of Lanae wiped out every sense of what was going on around him.

"What scares us?" Eric asked, laughing.

Moselle crossed to the door with a tray holding a coffee carafe surrounded by *Frivolities* mugs. She waited for Eric to open the slider.

Sage had yet to give Lanae a decent greeting.

Eric smacked Moselle with a tender kiss, and she shooed him away with a hip bump. Sage wondered if

Lezlie would ever find that kind of happiness. She'd dedicated many years to Jaxson. Followed by college, and now her nursing career.

Sage joined Rainn and Eric on the deck, where a cast iron chimenea that looked like a modern potbellied stove exuded welcoming heat. "Not quite like my fireplace, but I'll take it."

Silence wrapped around the men while they moaned over and devoured chocolate and cherry and some other kind of berry cheesecake slices. The women were clearly observed through the glass doors, deep in their own chatter. Lanae, in a bright emerald sweater and skinny jeans, glanced over her shoulder. He dropped his eyes to focus on the plate in his hand.

Sage eventually set his plate down and rubbed his stomach. He bypassed a comfortable oak rocker to rest against one of the porch columns. "So, Eric, Lanae said you built the deck?"

"Sure did. But Rainn helped."

"I'm impressed."

"I'm convinced digging those postholes was one of the ways I caught Geneva's eye." Rainn shot Sage a cheeky grin, followed by wiggling eyebrows. "Then again, maybe it's my looks."

They laughed, fell into another comfortable silence, and singled out their women through the glass patio doors.

"It's enterprising of them, for sure. Small business is sometimes a tough go in Nebraska, no matter what the economy is doing." Eric helped himself to an air-pot puff of steaming hot cider.

Lanae turned to catch them spying and shot him a smile that Sage felt in his stomach. He followed every step as she came to slide open the door. "So which one of you guys wants to pose for a plywood mannequin? We want to have a summer beanbag toss out back, and a little sandbox for kids."

"Mia would love that." Rainn lifted his mug in the air.

"It was her idea," Geneva added, joining her sister.

"Well, we don't want her tossing things at her dad's head, so Rainn's out," Moselle put in.

"Count me out, too," Eric added. "It isn't a good idea for kids to throw things at fireman. We save people from burning buildings."

They all looked at Sage.

"Gotta be a cowboy." Lanae shot him a saucy wink.

"Suppose I could. I've never been a model before. But wouldn't kisses be better than throwing things?" He made the last comment with his gaze locked on Lanae.

She blew him a kiss and closed the door.

If Lanae knew about Ted Tippin, she'd discover the news of Ted's father. And Sage wanted to keep everything about his Grandfather Earl, good and buried.

Rainn set his coffee mug on the serving tray, peered through the door, and appeared mesmerized as he watched Geneva. "Sometimes I can't get over the Lord bringing that woman into my life. And Mia into both our lives. I can hardly wait sometimes to get settled down together."

"Seems Rainn, my buddy here, kept it all to himself that he had an eye on Geneva as someone other than Moselle's mom." Eric said.

Sage wondered what it would be like to have a friend as close as Eric and Rainn appeared to be.

Maybe it was time he spent time with men instead of horses.

Rainn tore his gaze away from the scene inside the loft. "I guess we're supposed to be talking shop here, but—"

"Do the ladies have a website? My grandson's a tech whiz," Sage offered.

"They do, thanks," Eric answered.

Rainn cleared his throat. "I'm guessing Moselle will cover the list and its presentation with her usual pomp and creative style. Back to my subject. Sage, man, this *Frivolities* guy thing can wait. Since I'm all in love here, and Eric and I are of an age, I wanna know. Is there something about Lanae that gets to you? You know, makes her irresistible? I guess what I'm getting at, is it the same for a guy your age? Just wondering if I'll always feel this way about my woman."

Sage dropped the foot he'd propped against the square post. Standing tall, he leveled a dumbfounded stare at Rainn. They'd met a few minutes ago, and he sure wasn't used to sharing such private thoughts. He'd incorrectly stereotyped artists as quiet and unassuming.

Rainn stepped close to Sage to give him an elbow nudge and cocked a single brow. "When I was getting to know Geneva, and she was playing hard to get, Eric asked me what I dwelled on when I thought about her. She was about to become his mother-in-law, so I didn't say that she revs my motor. I told him it's her glasses. Every time she wears them I want to take them off."

Sage didn't laugh with them. He directed his gaze to Eric.

"OK. I'll bite." Eric ran his fingers down the grooves at the corners of his mouth. "Moselle's upper lip. She has this little mole above her lip. It just begs to be kissed. Your turn." Eric raised his mug in Sage's direction.

"Aren't we supposed to be helping the women with marketing ideas?"

Eric and Rainn didn't answer. Rather, they stared, and waited for Sage to respond.

"Looks like I'm outnumbered." Sage dry-spitted all ten of his fingers and mimed spiking his short hair. "Lanae's hair. I don't know why, but it just plain gets to me. I saw a picture of an older model on a tabloid while checking out at the grocery store not too long ago. Thought the woman had moxie. Then when I met Lanae, well, she's got the spunk to go along with the short, short hair..."

The three men sobered.

"OK, admit it. You think she's worth investigating." Rainn still searched Sage's face.

"In other words, age doesn't have a thing to do with man-woman connection," Eric concluded.

Sage had no time to agree or disagree with Eric's statement before Lanae swished through the door singing something about being out there then broke off. "Ideas, guys?"

She gave a curvy hip swing and changed her tune.

As though they had rehearsed it, each woman paraded after Lanae and went to her man—even Mia, who stood in front of Geneva while they both leaned back against Rainn.

Did Sage want to be Lanae's man? He couldn't take his eyes off her.

Rainn wrapped his arms around Geneva, settling a hand on Mia's shoulder. Eric folded his hands at the base of Moselle's ribcage.

Sage considered himself to be a nonconformist, but he couldn't pass up the chance to have his own arms full of intriguing femininity. All soft and curvy, Lanae smelled like cinnamon and chocolate. He turned her around so she could lean against him, and rested his chin lightly on the top of her head. He jerked back when Geneva opened up the conversation, eyes locked on her husband-to-be. "How do you like the deck, Sage? Rainn dug the holes for the posts."

Sage figured the heat from the stove was mild compared to the secret blast Geneva and Rainn sent one another with their eye contact.

"Hubba, hubba," Lanae added.

Sage envied the loving pleasure in her voice and wondered if she'd ever use that tone for him.

Lanae cleared her throat and angled her head to look up at him. "Back to ideas."

He glanced at the other couples. Moselle covered Eric's hands, rubbing a finger over his wedding band. Rainn and Geneva shared another special look, raising the outdoor temperature another five degrees.

Sage cleared his throat when his gaze met Lanae's. He settled his hands at her sides, feeling her woman shape.

"Before we hear suggestions for shopping, men, we have an idea. But I need your permission—"

More intrigued than ever, Sage held onto the connection with Lanae by a press of his hands.

"One of the letters I found isn't addressed to Ted like the others. Could we put it on display downstairs?"

As he considered, his gaze intent on her hazel eyes, he figured it couldn't hurt. It would give her something to do besides search for Ted Tippin. If he had to bend her over backward and kiss her until her brain melted, he'd do it to keep her from finding out the mysterious Ted was his uncle.

He'd be seeing Ms. Petersen on a regular basis. What could it hurt? And he'd enjoy every smack.

He nodded, giving assent to her question.

****

Life is about change. And being rearranged.

As much as Lanae wanted to incorporate a gentlemen's approach to *Frivolities*, they hadn't come up with much except a website link Moselle had started.

All evening, Lanae had the urge to shoo everyone away from the loft. She needed affirmation the women had selected the right letter to frame for display. Then again, they didn't matter in the decision. Sage had granted permission to use the undated one.

It was time to read all the letters in one sitting.

Lanae curled up with her favorite teal and mauve afghan, hot chocolate next to her chair, and opened each letter in turn.

An hour and a half later, she wiped away silent tears. The perfect letter to frame was the first one she'd read tonight, the letter with no date.

She read the undated words out loud once more.

Oh, how she felt for Katherine. What in the world had happened in the lives of these lovers?

Tears turned into a torrent.

She wept loud animal noises, wrapped her arms around her knees, and rocked.

Lanae knew Katherine's longing intrinsically. She

had mourned Keith to the very core of her being. For some reason, the holes felt new.

Loneliness widened a gap in Lanae's heart.

Oh, Lord, is Sage meant to fill these holes? You've given me a new lease on life. Forgive my discontent, my longing for something more. A life in the country is the desire of my heart. Which You know, because You know my heart.

10

Expect the unexpected – and enjoy it.

"I hate to admit it, but *Frivolities* seems to be the only place in town to buy decent gifts for other women," Kate Rawlins announced her grudging presence before the bell quit vibrating against the oak of the heavy front door. "I'm looking for a gift for my great-niece who's coming to visit Christmas Eve."

Why did the one customer in *Frivolities* have to be the town gossip? It bordered on rudeness, but Lanae wanted no distractions while she dissected and admired the latest creative efforts she shared with Geneva and Moselle.

The three owners greeted Kate in turn, knowing that she preferred snooping without assistance. They stood in a group, surveying their handiwork in the window display with three pairs of critical eyes.

Lanae patted herself on each shoulder, then gave Geneva and Moselle a loving touch, jubilant over the outcome of the snazzy vanity. Now the focus of a framed collage, the letter held Christmas court in the window, displayed on an easel leaning against a vanity leg.

Geneva's quilt sampler in a Victorian fan pattern, a crocheted doily of Lanae's atop a table runner, along with one of Moselle's *Frivolities* Memory Boxes sat on the vanity top, completing the attractive window presentation.

"I wonder if it was a mistake to use the only letter without a date," Moselle said.

"I believe Katherine wrote the letter before the last dated one, when she tells Ted that she is moving to Omaha," Lanae said.

At the sudden sound of shattered glass, the trio released a collective gasp.

Crystal fragments, once in the shape of a rose, lay in smithereens on the floor at Kate's feet.

Geneva and Lanae scurried to Kate's side.

"Don't worry about it," Geneva said.

At the sight of all the color leaching from Kate's face, Lanae asked, "Are you all right, Kate?"

Tremors shook Kate's frail body.

Moselle, being the youngest and fastest, grabbed Kate's arm to keep her from falling.

Kate yanked her arm free and rushed out the door, only to sag against the outside framework between door and window.

"I'll go." Lanae grabbed a magenta shawl, went outside and slung it over Kate's shoulders, fearful the woman could have a heart attack or burst something, judging by her lack of facial color.

Eyes glued on Kate's face, Lanae stayed close, where she stood as though frozen in place.

Kate stared through the window, her lower lip trembling. Her gaze traveled the cursive lines, and her lips moved as she silently read the words of the framed letter. Her breathing was heavy and shallow, even erratic. Her lower lip quivered and she choked. Tears flowed.

Kate took a step closer to the glass and clutched

her purse to her waist with both hands. Then her purse swished to the sidewalk in a soft rustling contrast to the earlier splintering glass. The quivering woman covered her mouth with her fists. Then they, too, sank as though dropped.

"I sent so many letters to my Teddy, so many years ago. He was my one true love."

"Katherine?" Lanae screamed the name in her mind, but it came out a whisper. Lanae would absorb the shock later.

Kate Rawlins appeared to be going into her own shock.

Lanae spoke her name three times, but Kate ignored her.

Familiarity with the contents of the letters made Lanae place a gentle hand on Kate's shoulders, to hold her close. The small, older woman shook in Lanae's arms.

"Let's go back inside, Kate. Where it's warm." She guided the woman toward the door.

Lanae wondered if they were in a dream, while she kept her own disbelief at bay.

"He disappeared, you know. My Teddy. Vanished into thin air." Kate sagged like a rag doll.

Lanae teetered under Kate's weight.

And fell through the open door to *Frivolities*.

****

"Whoa, there." Sage jerked in reaction when he opened the front door of *Frivolities* from the inside, surprised to find two unsteady women falling into him. He grabbed Lanae's upper arms, giving her balance in order to steady both women.

Sage set Lanae aside and bent to curl his arm around the skinny woman's knees, supported her against his chest with his other, and carried her through the shop.

"When I accepted that Teddy Tippin was never coming back to me..."

Sage felt his own knees go weak when he heard his uncle's name spoken out loud. He staggered, and pretended to swerve out of Moselle's way as she squeezed by them to open the office door at the back of the shop. The movement helped Sage hold the woman's mumbled words close to his chest.

He glanced up.

Moselle had disappeared through the office door.

Lanae's steps were interrupted when the phone rang.

Geneva was flying up the loft stairs.

Once assured none of the others had heard Ted's last name, he barreled on to the office.

"Katherine disappeared," the frail woman said.

Sage deposited her light weight in the corner of the sofa, placing a purple velvet pillow beneath her head. "I don't know who Katherine is, but these gals will take care of you."

"Thanks, Sage." Moselle nodded at him.

Then she knelt beside the sofa and gently patted the dangling arm before placing it on the woman's stomach. "Mom went to get a blanket."

Sage breathed easier as color returned to the woman's sunken cheeks. Her body quit its tremors.

The sprig of a woman kept mumbling in a soft, shaky voice. "I became Kate and worked as an insurance secretary in Omaha until my parents came down with a terrible influenza, so ill they needed me back home to run the bakery."

Sage stood aside so Lanae could hand a glass of water to the woman she addressed as Kate.

Lanae looked as emotional as Kate sounded, as though the older woman's story threatened to turn them both into blubbering globs.

"I moved to Platteville, and I never left again."

"Did you ever find out what happened?" Geneva asked from the doorway, handing a fleece blanket to Moselle.

"I never saw my Teddy again. And I've wondered all these years why I'm even alive." Silent tears streamed in a river down her face. "I've lived a lifetime of emptiness. I didn't really want to go on living without him."

Sage had to get out before he heard the woman repeat Ted's last name. Somehow, he hoped to keep that knowledge to himself.

"Sorry to show up at such a bad time. You women seem to have this under control." Sage knew the strong family would care for the older woman.

Moselle caught up with him at the back entrance. "Aunt Lanae's pretty shook up at the moment. To be honest, I'm a bit shaken myself. She tried so hard to discover who Katherine is, and then to have her just land in our laps, so to speak, is beyond weird."

Moselle fiddled with both earrings, as though checking to see if the silver feathers bobbed where she had put them. "Now I apologize. I came back to see if you wanted me to tell Aunt Lanae anything?"

"Nope. I picked up my new saddle, and I thought she might like to see it. Came through the alley door because I know she sometimes works back there. I'll catch you all another time." Sage left the way he had arrived. The alley door bounced open while he was trying to shut it.

"Sage, thank you! It was a God-thing, you appearing when I thought Kate and I would both topple over. It's stranger than fiction."

He let Lanae ramble, acting clueless.

"Poor Kate. Years ago, when Geneva told me about the way Kate kept gossip alive regarding Moselle and Eric's high school history, I figured she was a busybody with nothing better to do. Labels can be so wrong. I never considered Kate had a reason to be so unhappy. Her life ended when her dear Ted disappeared."

And my mother's life became new once she was free from my grandfather's abuse.

When Lanae looked deep into Sage's eyes with such trust, he had to turn away. He was unable to put a description to what he read on her face, but it was all female emotion. This particular female wanted things he couldn't give.

She hugged him quick and released him. "We'll talk later, OK?" And then she shut the door.

Sage didn't want to get wrapped up in it. He wasn't used to so much drama. He had to sort this all out, get it straight in his mind. Yet he knew it was only a matter of time before Lanae, and Lezlie, for that matter, discovered the truth.

11

The only way to stop fear is to pass it up on the way to a successful life.

Lanae spoke before Lezlie finished answering her phone. "I have Ted's last name! It's Tippin. I can hardly wait to run a Google search. And would you believe, Katherine, the letter writer, is someone we know! In fact, she's Kate Rawlins, the woman most of Platteville considers the town gossip." She paused to give Lezlie a chance to respond.

"That's great. I could go online tonight if you like."

"Since this involves your family, sure. Go for it! I'm kind of feeling off, maybe I used too much energy over all the excitement we had in the shop earlier. Your dad was here and carried poor Kate through to the office. I thought she was going to collapse."

"He gets around. Suppose his saddle's finished."

"That's exactly why he stopped, according to Moselle, to show off his new saddle. But in all the confusion, he made a hasty retreat."

They shared a laugh and Lezlie added, "Dad doesn't do well with tearful women in crisis."

"I guessed as much. So do you know Ted Tippin? Is he related to you?"

"For some reason the name rings a distant bell.

Dad's always been closemouthed about his family, though. I can hardly wait to check it out. Sounds like some kind of family skeleton in the closet."

"Family secrets have a way of coming out eventually, even if they miss a generation or two." Lanae waited a beat, but the younger woman made no comment. She'd heard once that people's lives were affected by what their ancestors did while alive.

Sage must have a family secret.

Lanae bid Lezlie a hasty good-bye.

She retied her *Frivolities* apron strings, and tried to find something to tidy or straighten in the window where the vanity held court. But it looked perfect.

Except for turning Kate Rawlins' life upside down. *And mine.*

She considered Kate's unfulfilled longing for a life with her Ted.

And remembered the way Sage had scooped Kate up.

Her breathing and pulse rate quickened. With all of her heart, Lanae wanted to be held safe in Sage's arms. She closed her eyes, imagined him sweeping her off her feet, tucked in snug against the pounding of his heart.

Lord, like it or not, my secret longing is for Sage. I'm more and more aware of the reawakening passionate side of my nature. I want Sage, but I don't know if Sage is what You want for me.

All our lives are in Your hands, Lord. If some dark secret is about to emerge, please give us all the grace to see it through, especially Sage.

Geneva and Moselle were somewhere. Lanae took advantage of the quiet due to the lack of customers. She left the door open so she could hear the bell above the front door and wove her way up the meandering painted vines on the loft steps. From a shelf of the cabinet next to her recliner, she dug out one of her copied letters, tucked away inside a quilted book jacket Geneva had made.

As heartrending as the whole day had been, with Kate falling to pieces over sight of the letter and remembering Ted's disappearance, hadn't her own heartstrings been torn up enough?

Yet she chose to read.

July 5, 1960
Tuesday 4 a.m.

Dearest Teddy,

Isn't it something that Hawaii is our 50th state now? Are we living history or what?

I can't imagine why you would stand me up.
I'm frantic with worry.
These weeks not getting to be with you, I'm sick inside.
I even got brave enough to make a long distance call to your house, but there was no answer, just a lot of clicks on the party line from your neighbors. Can't they let a person have a call of their own?
Please, please, let me know that you are all right.

Be good, Sweet. Lots of love and kisses.
xxxxxxxxxxxxxxxxxxxxxxxxxxxxxxxxxxxxxxxxxxxxxxxx

Katherine

P.S. (Or maybe you aren't so dear at the moment.)

****

Sage stood at the mantle in his great room, holding the silver framed photograph of Becca. Life felt all off kilter again, the way it had after he'd lost her.

"I wish you were here to help me sort this all out. I'd have to tell you the story first. And, baby, I did keep it from you."

He ran his thumb over the image of her deep red hair, the glass feeling cold and lifeless. Sage set the picture back in place. He picked up his coffee mug from the side table between the dark brown leather recliner and couch, but the coffee was cold.

At loose ends, he stared out the window.

Pictures. He had real-life photographs of his wife, but he carried around a mental picture of Uncle Ted. One of the things he remembered most was the way Ted Tippin peeled his oranges. No one else in the world, to Sage's knowledge, peeled their oranges that way.

There was a definite, unexplained ritual to the procedure including the way his uncle had folded kitchen linen to catch the juice. He used a handmade pearl-handled paring knife, always the same one, to section the peel before removing it. Once the peel was lifted from the orange, Uncle Ted proceeded to remove every seed, every vein, and every tiny piece of pulp, to leave only the meat of each section.

Later, after his mother had talked about the abuse at the hands of Ted's father, Sage had always figured that precise way of peeling an orange was Uncle Ted's way of taking his father apart, piece by piece.

The ringing phone interrupted his musings, and Sage snagged the mug of cold coffee on his way to the kitchen.

"Dad, Lanae called about Ted Tippin. I know I've heard the name before, maybe when I was a really little girl. Is he someone in our family?"

And there it was. Finally out in the open.

He tossed the coffee into the sink, wishing he could toss away bitterness so easy. "Yeah. I guess it's time I spilled some of the past. It'll solve nothing at this point. And it'll leave a bad taste in your mouth."

"I'll come out later. Can I bring anything?"

"Not a thing. On second thought, maybe Jax. That way I won't have to tell the story a second time."

Two hours later, he opened the door to welcome not only his family, but Lanae, who followed Lezlie and Jaxson up the drive.

Sage had no time to figure out what he thought about Lanae's unannounced intrusion.

Lezlie answered before he asked. "I'm not sorry, Dad. She's part of this because she found our family letters."

He leaned down for Lezlie's kiss and a beat later, accepted the covered dish Lanae handed him. With his hands occupied, she kissed him. Smack dab on the lips. Smack dab in front of his daughter and grandson, leaving Sage speechless.

She turned her attention to Jaxson.

Lezlie made the introductions. "Lanae, this is my son, Jaxson."

"I would have known you right off, pleased to meet you. Hope you like cheesecake as much as your granddad. I've got a peanut butter one with chunks of candy bar on top."

Jaxson's blush deepened. Under different circumstances, Sage would have kidded his grandson.

Lanae stumbled through the door, more as if she was ill rather than losing her footing.

"Hey. You OK? I'd hate to drop the goods here to catch you."

"I'm fine. Fatigued is all. Achy joints and muscles. Figure some weather is coming in. I can't help but remember the headaches, stress, and appetite fluctuations that were sure signs of an over-worked liver."

Sage scowled. "What are you talking about? And why are you here if you're sick?"

"It's not like I'm contagious. I'm taking some herbals to ward off anything." She whipped out a small bottle of hand sanitizer. "And I have this in case you all think I might have something."

"Becca had enough sickness to last me a lifetime. Are you sure you're cured?"

"Cured of what?" Jaxson wanted to know.

"Hepatitis C," Lanae said, finally taking the covered container back from Sage, who gladly handed it over in exchange for their coats.

He caught Lanae looking at Lezlie for direction.

Lezlie led their guest to the kitchen side of the long granite-covered counter that divided the expansive room's living area.

Acting nervous, Lanae continued to talk while the women served the dessert. "Hepatitis C is usually contracted years before symptoms show, so we walk around without a clue that we can be dead men and women walking." She glanced at Sage then included them all. "I'm sorry if this touches a nerve. Anyway, when we do know why we're sick, we live up on the mountain top one moment and down in the deep valley next, grieving for our health just like we do when we lose a loved one." Lanae again met his gaze, offering a challenge without words.

"You know," Sage spoke up. "We've got enough to talk about tonight without details of your illness. I've told you before. I don't have room in my life for another sick woman."

"Dad, behave." Lezlie handed him a plate with three slivers of different cheesecakes.

"It's fine. Illness causes people to react in different ways, but..." Lanae's voice trailed off.

Sage made an effort to relax his tense facial muscles.

"Praise God, Sage, I'm healed now. My body didn't fall to the disgusting disease. And I take homeopathic medicines to keep my liver healthy. I'll probably take them for the rest of my life, just to make sure."

"It was tough watching Mom fade away," Lezlie said softly. "She suffered horribly. Maybe we don't talk about it enough."

Sage hugged Lezlie in passing. His daughter liked to view things from all perspectives.

"You don't talk about stuff," Jaxson said, rolling a huge bite of cheesecake around in his mouth. "I hardly know anything about when Grandma was sick."

Sage had one agenda for the evening. "Nobody came out here to talk about Becca. I've got another family situation to get out into the open."

"I'll end my part of this unpleasantness. I've forgotten to eat on a regular basis." Lanae blazed a smile at the Diamonds in turn. "I really will be fine. After a good night's rest."

She put an explanation point on her statement when she plopped a white chocolate curl onto her tongue. She licked chocolate off her finger, holding Sage's gaze throughout. Then she blotted her lips with the back of her hand, turned to wash at the sink before running a tall glass of water from the tap.

Earthy, yet all female. Sage couldn't help but watch her at-home woman-in-the-kitchen movements. But he wouldn't be distracted. He had to spill dirt from the past. Yet he scowled at Lanae.

Lanae spoke between sips of water. "Let's be done with it."

Sage figured Lanae was trying to lighten the tension so he could go about his disclosure. "Let's all find a seat."

He gave them a moment, not a whit surprised that Lanae followed him around the counter and chose to sit next to him on the deep cushions of the dark brown leather couch.

Jaxson bounded into the recliner, and Lezlie perched to attention on the stone hearth.

Sage spoke to the image smiling from the mantel, wishing he had told Becca the story while she lived. "Tippin is my mother's maiden name. Her dad's name was Earl. My grandmother's name was Juanita, and the dresser belonged to her before she gave it to my mother, Violet."

His unsteady hand rattled the fork against the plate. "My uncle's name is Ted. Ted Tippin."

Lanae gasped.

Sage set his plate down, no more appetite for anything. What he really wanted to do, but couldn't, was pull Lanae in close to his side. He could use a little warmth when his heart felt so cold and bitter. But this whole revelation was Lanae's fault.

"My mother said my Grandpa Earl was tough. And a mean old coot." Sage fisted his hands on his thighs. "I never saw that side of him, maybe because he'd mellowed by the time I came around. But he liked to be rough on his family, verbally abusive to the women. Physically to my uncle Ted. He'd been a blacksmith all his life and had arms bigger than my thighs."

He cleared his throat, wishing he was outside riding. Anywhere but here. He settled his gaze on the image of Becca. "Granddad was murdered on July Fourth, 1960. The same day Uncle Ted disappeared."

12

Life is tough. But with the grace of God, I'm tougher.

Lanae's face felt swollen from tears that had fallen throughout the emotional day. Sage's revelation started the waterworks all over again.

She now stood in silence, longing for her own familial hugs, while Sage bid his daughter and grandson goodnight.

Lezlie had also cried over her father's family revelation. She wiped tears away when she squeezed Sage. They exchanged cheek kisses. Sage kept an arm over her shoulders.

Poor Sage. He'd surely had his limit of tearful women for the day. First Kate, then Lezlie, now she felt like a blubbering mess.

She chuckled when Sage ruffled Jaxson's hair before pulling him into a side embrace. They prepared to leave.

The threesome filed through the door into the crisp, black night.

More tears threatened Lanae when the loneliness hit. She had no immediate family of her own, only Geneva and Moselle. Both of them had someone to love, and to love them in return.

Sage was so blessed. But did he realize it, or did he prefer to focus on his loss of Becca?

Through the window, Lanae could see Jaxson drop his chin and smooth the hair Sage had mussed. No one grinned or said anything flippant about the teen's actions, a clear testimonial as to how each adult was caught up in his or her own thoughts.

Sage crossed the threshold to return inside then stepped back outside. "Watch out for deer, honey."

Lanae lifted her crocheted poncho from the coat rack as Sage closed the door.

"Wait." Sage took the wrap from her hands. "Stay a while, please?"

Why would he want her to stay?

"I could use some company." He answered her question as though he'd read her mind.

Lanae had the impression Sage had held something back while revealing the literal skeleton-in-the-closet of the Tippin family. Would he tell her more family secrets?

"I'll stay if you agree to show me the rest of your lovely home."

She'd had a hard time reading Sage all evening. While sitting close to him on the sofa, she sensed him reaching out to her on some invisible level, yet his gaze had riveted on the image of his dead wife.

At the moment, in the quiet of her heart, lay an assurance that God wanted her and Sage to share an earthly destiny.

With obvious reluctance, he wanted her there.

She padded across the earth-toned area rug of the great room to gaze at the picture that graced the mantle shelf. Firelight brought golden cheeks to the woman in the photograph. "She's lovely. Except for her eyes, Lezlie is the spitting image."

With her peripheral vision, she saw Sage nod.

Judging by the way he'd stared at the picture while he talked about the Tippin family, Lanae guessed Sage opened up to Becca's picture a lot.

Her physical reminders of Keith were all tucked away.

Sage spoke after a brief silence filled only by the swishing dishwasher. "First, I apologize for my bluntness earlier. A chunk of my heart is missing. Most of the time I think I'll never be whole again. For a long time after she was gone, I imagined Becca in another room of the house. Then I'd search her out to find the room empty."

"That's normal. I did the same thing after Keith was killed. In fact, I kept the sheets on the bed for a month just so I could inhale his scent. I held on to his clothes for six months. Then one day I realized I couldn't smell him anymore."

"I kept a bottle of Becca's perfume. It put me in a depression for days every time Lezlie opened it to keep in touch with her mother's favorite scent."

Lanae, at a loss for words, headed for the stairs. She wanted to understand. Yet she wanted to pound something—like Sage's broad chest—and say, "Get over it already!"

But she knew from experience people grieved and moved on according to their own process.

During the first-floor tour, Lanae was most struck by the handcrafted furniture in the bedrooms. The headboards of the sturdy looking beds, the nightstands, and in one room, even a corner table with matching chair, were all constructed of pine. It looked as though the tree branches had been lobbed off to leave the trunks for construction. The chests of drawers and one dresser were fronted with cedar.

"I am so impressed, Sage. I'd like to be snowed in here so I can enjoy your furniture. It is lovely, like being in a rain washed forest glade."

"Thanks. I like it. Especially 'cause it's so different from the girly stuff Becca was into."

Becca. She couldn't escape the deceased wife.

Down the stairs, a five-by-five deer mount startled a gasp from Lanae. "You hunt, Sage?"

"Nah. That guy's a leftover from the previous owner, which surprises me. He was a vet."

She scanned the room where he obviously spent time. A worn, wide-ribbed corduroy couch in burnt orange angled so the watcher had the best view of a huge flat-screen television that took up most of the darkest wall. A beautiful antique cedar chest was covered with horse magazines, a giant mug with the design obliterated by age, and a library book.

One item Lanae hadn't seen in the house was a Bible.

She'd have to think about that. The man wasn't crass, didn't appear to treat women like doormats. The gentle way Sage had with horses and the way he loved his family exhibited Christian character. But exactly what kind of relationship did Sage have with the Lord?

Lanae shook her head over her wandering mind. A lower level walk-out to the east drew her close. "Oh, I'll bet this is lovely in the mornings."

"It is. The elevation right here is a little low, but the colors of the sky are still visible as the sun rises over the hill."

"What about animals? Do they wander up from the creek?"

"Oh, yeah." His chuckle filled her with warmth.

"Including little rascals, like 'coons and opossums.

But the deer make up for it. Early this past spring a young buck, going into velvet, came meandering up."

"Velvet's before the antlers harden?"

"Right. Then once, back in late summer when I was messing with rocks in the flower bed, I had my back to the field out there on the other side of the creek. A rumbling 'moo' sound came from behind me. First thought I had was the neighbor's cows must be out."

Sage's relaxed pleasure over nature's offering lit up his face. "I turned to find a large doe looking right at me, ears straight up in silhouette."

"Oh."

"'Well, hello there, sweetheart,'" I said to her in a low voice. 'There's room for both of us here,' I went on to tell her."

Lanae held back the urge to giggle at his exaggerated cowboy drawl.

"Did she listen?"

"She made her vocal noise once more. I've thought of it since, but so far haven't been able to put a descriptive word to the sound the doe made. And I've been unable to mimic the sound. We just stood there looking at one another, her ears poked straight up and her white tail straight down."

"What a thrill that had to have been."

"I told her thanks for talking to me. And it's all right for us to share this place."

Lanae looked to the dormant grassy area Sage indicated with a lift of his arm. The full moon gave the landscape an eerie, yet luminescent glow, a different sky than when she'd looked out earlier.

"The best was yet to come," Sage continued his tale. "She growled and stepped away, full of grace, at a loping walk. Then the doe turned to look back at me, grumbled once more. Her tail went up and twitched before she walked another ten feet or so."

He grinned, tanned lines accenting his fabulous eyes. "That doe made my day. It was one of those suspended-in-time moments."

My day and night have been made by you, Sage. How many days will we have together?

"But my day hadn't been complete until a fawn wearing its spots rose from the grass across the creek."

She couldn't resist. She gave him a quick hug before stepping back to tease him a little. "Ah. She wasn't talking to you, but to her baby."

She tried to decipher the emotion that turned his eyes such an silver in the moonlight. The weakness started in Lanae's stomach and traveled to her knees.

"Sage?" His name blew a whisper above a breath.

She leaned toward him.

He read the message in her eyes, and came closer with opened arms.

Lanae wanted Sage.

She wanted to reach inside him and pull him close. She wanted his mouth on hers. She wanted to feel him, to breathe him in. She wanted to taste him. To smell him. She wanted all of him.

Her knees wobbled when she remembered the heroic, yet tender manner in which Sage had carried Kate Rawlins through *Frivolities*.

Her head rolled back.

His head leaned forward.

This time, her name whooshed from his lips as a sigh, a beat before their lips finally met.

Somehow, with all the tumultuous shattering of her insides, she was suddenly calm with the rightness of it all. She might laugh later at her own contradiction, being calm and all riled up at once.

The kiss was more than a kiss. It was a release.

Her loneliness, her longing, her desire, all poured through with the heightened pressure of Sage's lips on hers.

He drew her tighter against him, as though he answered her silent pleas with wants as deeply buried as hers.

She hadn't felt so small, so secure, or so protected in a long, long time.

Intense, pent-up yearnings threatened to begin the weeping all over again.

She protested at the sudden assault on her senses, and a moan formed in her mind but didn't escape her lips. Sensations attacked her whole body, yet she was aware of each one. Her eyes drifted shut, and she closed out the world, subliminally exposing to Sage what he was awakening in her.

He smelled so good, like maple syrup and chocolate. And the tiniest hint of spice. Sage.

She imagined the scene he had described and wanted to be outside in the warm sunlight. She wanted the breeze to whisper over her skin. She longed to feel the sun warm her, to drive away the chill of all sickness.

More than anything, she wanted to let him know God was watching over them the way the doe protected her fawn. She wanted him to believe and trust God's purpose in taking Becca when He did. She hoped the next time Sage tended his garden in the sunlight, he saw God through the nature He provided.

And she wanted to share the great outdoors with Sage in his country life.

Her whimper escaped, loud in the quiet room.

Sage groaned and drew back, holding the tiniest piece of her bottom lip gently between his teeth as though he was reluctant to break their intimate connection.

He raised his head, but held hers in the palm of his hand, and nudged her against his chest. She closed her eyes and nestled her ear near his heart. They stood without stirring while their breathing and pulse rates returned to normal.

Normal? Not on your life.

He pulled back with a start as though coming to after getting bucked off a horse.

"That shouldn't have happened." His voice was gruff. "You'd better go."

What happened to her gentle horse whisperer? Becca must have entered his thoughts.

Lanae had counted six pictures of the woman in question, all propped in prominent places throughout the ranch home.

Did Sage mean to give her the subliminal message his one true love reigned in his house?

Was that message enough to keep Sage from Lanae's heart?

Too late. He was already there.

And it appeared Sage would stay in her heart rather than her life. *As long as he still loved Becca.*

It was right there in his eyes.

Sage was full of contradictions in the vibes he'd put off throughout the evening. Did he even recognize his conflicted thinking? He hadn't let his dead wife go.

And it appears he's unwilling to take on another diseased woman. Even if I am healed.

"It is time for me to go. Tonight was emotional for

all of us. I'll see myself out."

She started up the staircase and waited for him to step close behind. At the top of the stairs he turned to her, where they stood at the end of the hallway before re-entering the great room.

"Watch out for deer."

He may have shut her out, but he cared enough to repeat the same warning he'd given Lezlie.

Lanae smiled in the darkness. Would he ever address her as "honey?"

And why in the world did some men apologize for a kiss?

****

July 12, 1960
4:30 a.m.

Darling Ted,
Where are you?
Your mother finally answered the telephone, and she sounded as sick as I feel for you inside. And I can understand that.

Oh, Ted, I'm so sorry your father is dead, and in such a tragic way.

On the Fourth of July, no less.

There is so much talk about what happened.

Do you think it was a hobo passing through?

I so wonder where you were when it happened. Not making it to your own father's funeral, people are talking about that, too, even here in Platteville.

But the old saying is "you never miss the water until the well goes dry." And I have missed you that much, dear.

Last night I couldn't get to sleep for thinking about you and what has happened to your family.

Your poor mother. Your poor sisters.

It was past 2:00 a.m. when I finally fell asleep, only to wake an hour later. I can't imagine where you are, sweetheart. I feel like life isn't real right now.

Well, honey, I am not going to write much anymore. So, bye, bye, dearest, until we meet again.

Be good, sweet. Lots of love and kisses. xxxxxxxxxxxxxxxxxxxxxxxxxxxxxxxxxxxxxxxxxxxxxxxxx xxxxxxxxxxxxxxxxxxxxxxxxxxxxxxxxxxxxxxxxxxxxxxxxxx xxxxxxxxxxxxxxxx

Lovingly,
Katherine

Lanae didn't even attempt to swipe at the silent tears washing her cheeks. "Not the thing to read right before bed."

She followed Katherine's written example, unable to sleep. After tossing for an hour, Lanae got up and went down the stairs to the *Frivolities* office. Once logged on, she searched Nebraska's unsolved homicides on the Internet.

Nothing more than what Sage had told them. Only a listing in a newspaper article from years before, naming a state trooper who was assigned to cold cases.

No hits. Evidently the case of Earl Tippin was far too cold.

Lord, I seek the joy that only You can provide. Please help me be content in where You have me right now.

Maybe, someday, she'd look back and be thankful for the way Sage had made her feel so alive.

Someday.

Right now life felt like a roll of yarn unraveled by a naughty kitten. And the closer it got to the end, the faster it rolled.

"Can I end my days in happiness having known Sage? Will I thank the Lord for letting us meet?"

And why have I been exposed to country life again?

Could she get through to Sage by following Kate's example and writing him a letter? Would it be easier to get her feelings down on paper, where he'd have something other than Becca before his eyes?

She reached for pen and tablet.

The middle of a December night

Dear Sage,

Thank you for the deer warning. I was within spitting distance of your driveway, when a voice, probably my guardian angel, or the Spirit of the Lord, said "slow down." It was so strange. Through my mind's eye, I saw a doe bound from the field on my right seconds before she appeared. Does that make sense? She darted out of nowhere, but I was going slow enough that she crossed the road while I was braking, so we both escaped a nasty outcome. I was pretty shaken, though, and couldn't settle down to sleep when I tried to get comfy.

I looked out the sliding glass doors of the loft, into the dark, early December night. The air is definitely growing frostier. The sky is all gray and cloudy, but the beautiful moon shone bright earlier. The first snow has got to be around the corner. Can you feel it, too?

For some reason I had a flash of memory from a night on the ranch. Sometimes I mourn the loss of the ranch as much as I do the loss of Keith. That's so stupid, really, considering the blessings I have found here with Geneva and

Moselle and Frivolities.

And now meeting you and your family.

Sage, thank you also, for including me in your revelation to Lezlie and Jaxson. That must have been so difficult for you. I can't imagine facing July Fourth each year with that kind of unresolved family history.

Love,

Lanae

P.S. I do love you. You can take it as a free gift, or you can leave it in my heart where it will never grow to fruition, as long as you remain in love with a dead woman.

A tear dropped with a splat on the back of Lanae's hand. If she found the nerve to send the letter, she'd leave off the postscript. Then again, maybe not.

Would she be content if Jesus remained the lover of her soul?

Knowing He was there as part of who she was didn't mean it brought contentment to Lanae's heart. Contentment came from spiritual growth.

Looked like she had some growing to do.

13

I refuse to be an old lady who says, "If I had my life to live over I would do such-and-such."

The following morning, Lanae rose early, feeling like she moved in a dream, she was so sleep deprived. And achy. But she fought going there, recalling the way she used to wake up. When she rose, she'd search for signs of jaundice in her mirrored image. Often her pinkish eyelids looked as though she'd brushed on shadow.

"Why are you going there, woman? Think about the cowboy all alone on his acreage," she admonished herself in the empty bathroom.

Oh yeah, it had felt so right to be held close by Sage, with all those muscles and his masculine strength surrounding her. Filling her up with how things could be.

If I don't live my life to the fullest, there is no one else to live it for me. And I want to share my life with Sage.

But he was still in love—even though she was gone.

Daydreaming about Sage, Lanae soaped her underarms. She set aside the shaving gel and grabbed her shaver. Rinsing off, left arm upraised, she jerked and fast came out of her dream state. The bristles jabbed. "What in the world?"

She burst out laughing, and snatched her shaver off the rim of the tub again. So preoccupied with thoughts of Sage, she didn't know what she was doing. She soaped up but hadn't shaved. "It's come to this? Not only talking to myself, but pulling off Geneva antics?"

Geneva once had Lanae rolling with laughter when she'd described creaming up one smooth leg only to discover she had forgotten to shave the other. All because she'd been thinking about Rainn.

Lanae removed the plastic cover from her shaver, a newly established safety precaution with Mia around, and attended to the business of hair removal.

A short time later, she spoke to her baking utensils as she gathered cheesecake ingredients. "I love you, Sage. I know you don't want me to."

She was in the mood to bake. The cakes lasted in the freezer nicely until needed in Frivolities.

She could hear Sage answer something like, "That's right. You had your love in Keith. I've loved Becca. I still love Becca."

Would he be that honest?

Would she be brave enough to mail the letter?

At the sight of her baking chocolates lined up in a row—white, dark, milk—she decided to use two-tone chocolate for curls. Sage claimed to love dark chocolate.

She got all fluttery inside at the recollection of savoring his tasty kisses, the way she'd melted like chocolate in his embrace.

She had no idea which flavors she'd end up with, so she also set out chocolate chips, along with nuts and a variety of flavorings. She grabbed a can of pumpkin pie mix and added the peanut butter jar. She wasn't in the mood for fruit or berries today. Lanae danced around her kitchenette and pictured the long counter in Sage's home. "Now, that's the place to do some serious baking."

Just that fast, inert, she bowed her head.

Thank You, Lord. Thank You for giving me the energy to cook. For so long I couldn't think of or even taste and appreciate food. Thanks for giving me restored health.

Lanae opened her eyes and turned on her mixer, singing, "Jesus Loves Me."

The beaters churned and rhyming words flitted through her mind: burn, churn, fern, learn, stern, yearn.

Next, Lanae thought of Katherine. Rather, Kate Rawlins, and the impact Kate's written yearning for her Teddy had on Lanae's own emotions.

No doubt about it, Lanae yearned for Sage. And she could love Sage with every fiber of her being if he would open up and let her in.

"Is that what you want, Lord? I can't help but think Sage and I wouldn't have met if You didn't want us to be together."

And I could live in the country again, where I belong.

She went through the rest of the day wondering how Kate fared. By the time *Frivolities* was locked up for the night, Lanae had determined to take half a cheesecake to Kate.

"Not that we could be friends or anything, but I can't help but feel sorry for her," she told Geneva when they bid one another goodnight. "I want to check up on her."

She also didn't want to confess to her sister that she was drawn to Sage through the letters. Somehow she empathized with Kate's loneliness through her own yearning for Sage.

Lanae was so churned up inside that she imagined herself unraveling, one stitch at a time, like the loops of a life-long crocheted scarf.

****

Sage thumped the heel of his right hand into the palm of his left, tried to focus on the words booming from his fifty-inch flat-screen downstairs. Then he yanked the remote control off the cedar chest he used for a coffee table. "Me, me, me. This world is not all about the likes of you!"

The talking head kept on smiling and yakking after he muted the talk show guest. "Can't these people find something worthwhile to talk about besides their shallow lives and their stupid secrets?"

Disgusted with himself for even sitting there in the middle of the day, he hit the power button on the remote. All day he'd been out of sorts, especially inside the house. He couldn't figure out what was wrong.

He stormed upstairs and circled the kitchen, grabbed his outer wear, and almost ran through the garage.

On his way to the barn, the chilly humidity hit him with a harsh reminder that winter was closing in. He had to check on those Florida condo-on-the-beach reservations. A lot of ocean sun should warm the achy Nebraska chill from his bones.

It'd be a nice night for cuddlin'.

That thought stopped him in his tracks.

Only one woman came to mind with the idea of cuddling. Lanae Petersen. She could be opinionated. She sure was stubborn, going after the mystery behind the letters, but he had to admire her as well. She was a survivor, and went after what she wanted from life.

Could she want him?

Sage recalled their first real kiss. Lanae had tasted just as he had supposed. He remembered the way her sweetness lingered, as though he were a horse drawn to the delicacy of sweet spring grasses.

Somewhere along the line, he'd left his intention behind. He'd wanted Lanae to focus on him instead of her search for Ted. She'd hooked him instead. Ever since he kissed her, he'd replaced talking to Becca with a preoccupation of holding lively Lanae.

He studied his surroundings. The air had the damp, crisp feel of snow, and the sky was white with clouds. He remembered how Lanae, in her skinny jeans, had fit right in on his land.

Sage strode on.

He didn't want Lanae to want him, yet he couldn't stomach the idea of her wanting any other man.

Even if he wanted her in return, no way could he waste his time on another woman with an illness. He lacked that kind of tough hide.

When he slid open the barn door, soft horse nickers greeted him.

"How-do, everybody. I got a little lonely all by myself and figured you could use some company, too, so I came out to say hello."

He swept the jacket hood off his cap, readjusted the bill. Lonely. He'd actually said it out loud.

Suddenly, a sharp reminder of the Christmas story came to mind. Mary and Joseph must have been greeted by the same kind of animal warmth long ago on that historic Bethlehem night.

Why did God have to bring Jesus into the picture

of his turmoil? He liked being alone.

Didn't he?

"I gave my heart once, God. And you took my Becca. I don't want Lanae or any other woman getting in there again. Especially a woman with a history of being sick."

I'll be fine with Lezlie and Jaxson, thanks anyway.

Sage stroked Freckles between the eyes, slapped his hand gently down the length of the soft neck, and tickled with his fingers under the large, warm belly.

And he remembered watching Lanae do the same thing.

At the time, he'd had a gut reaction as though he were the recipient of those talented fingers. Wherever Lanae's hands had brushed the horse, Sage had felt his own skin quiver with the imagined impression of her touch on his skin.

Right now Sage felt like a horse trotted along the trail of his insides, kicking up gravel and slinging all kinds of debris.

He'd been perfectly fine with his life the way it was. Before that woman punched his phone number and changed his life.

Now that he'd met her, how could he survive leaving Nebraska knowing he'd be leaving Lanae behind?

****

Lanae's sedan tires spun some as she rooted for traction after putting the car in Drive. By the time she parked next to Kate's little house, she knew she'd better have her ice scraper handy before driving back to the loft. The air was heavy with cold crystals of moisture. The moon wouldn't show its face anytime soon.

She had yet to consider the loft as "home." Platteville was home. Geneva's two-story frame house with the front porch, swing and all, she had considered home. But for some reason when she thought of the loft, it still belonged to Moselle. Eric's skilled carpentry had lovingly prepared the loft as an extension of *Frivolities*, an expression of his love for Moselle.

Sage hadn't been on his acreage long—five years, if she remembered right. Did he consider it home? Probably. Yet Becca was there with him.

Shake it off.

Kate Rawlins lived at the opposite end of Platteville from Geneva. Her one-story bungalow appeared on the shabby side, even after sundown. Lanae eased herself out of the sedan and reached back in for the plate of cheesecake she had covered and topped off with a Christmas bow.

The woman looked eighty when she answered Lanae's knock. Kate's eyes appeared sunken, lacking the light of life.

"Hi, Kate." Lanae smiled in greeting. "I brought you some peppermint cheesecake and wanted to make sure you were doing all right after your shock yesterday."

"Oh, how thoughtful." Kate stood there after her remark as though she didn't know what to do next.

"May I take it to your kitchen?"

"How thoughtless of me. Of course. Please. Come in." Kate stepped aside and slowly shut the door once Lanae walked through.

Lanae waited but received no more direction from Kate. When she was a vibrant Katherine, Lanae imagined the spark of youth, of love, had shone from Kate's eyes.

Now Kate wore a lackluster look, like the spark of life had abandoned her. Her usual red lipstick was missing. Her skin looked gray in the dim front-room light.

"I'll just take this on back, then." Lanae strode through the small room, careful not to trip on a corner of the ragged rug rolled up on the kitchen side of the threshold.

A fluorescent light over the sink revealed spotless counters. No cooking smells spiced the stale, dead-scented air.

"Kate, have you eaten yet tonight?"

Lanae glanced back to see Kate Rawlins, unmoving, next to the front door. Her heavy gray sweater listed off one sagging shoulder.

"Uh, no. I've been resting most of the day."

"I've done that myself. Not healthy for anyone. I'll guess you haven't eaten since morning. Do you have a can of soup? Or would you rather I fix you a sandwich?"

"Please, don't bother—"

"No bother whatsoever. I miss having someone to fuss over."

Lanae set to work. First, she opened the refrigerator and set the cheesecake inside, noting bare essentials like milk, butter, bread, cheese, and bruised fruit in a crisper drawer. She grabbed what she needed, including a wrinkled apple. Next, she opened cupboard doors and transferred necessities for grilled cheese and tomato soup.

Once she got busy with the light meal preparation, she observed Kate.

Kate shuffled a step closer to the kitchen, and Lanae caught glimmers of the single life of an elderly woman. No shine to it. But without *Frivolities*, or crocheting for the babies in hospitals and shelters, that single life may not have been that far ahead in Lanae's future.

By the time Kate sank onto a kitchen chair, tailbone rigid, Lanae resolved to never end up this way. No music. Muted television. Rumpled cover over sunken couch cushions. Few comforts were evident, other than two more throws and three family photographs on the wall. Only a Bible and water-stained coaster sat isolated on the junky antique coffee table.

Lanae served Kate the simple meal. Then she put water on to heat for tea before taking a seat at the small table covered in the only colorful spot in the kitchen. The faded red poinsettias on the tablecloth were the lone sign of Christmas Lanae noted in Kate's home.

"Would it help to talk more about Ted and your letters to him, Kate?"

"My manners are normally better." Kate's chest rose with a quivery sigh. "Thank you, Lanae, for your kindness. Are you sure you want nothing to eat?"

"I'm fine." Lanae smiled, watching Kate test the heat of the soup, then daintily slurp two spoonfuls.

The kettle whistled. Lanae went about the makings of tea for them both; and by the time she sat back down, Kate wore rosy cheeks. She scootched to the back of the chair and chewed her last bite of sandwich.

"I've done enough thinking about Teddy to last three old-maid lifetimes. I talked enough about him yesterday to make you depressed. Your coming here has revived me more than I can say."

Lanae stroked the older woman's forearm where it rested on the table. "How about some cheesecake to go with that tea?"

"Oh, I'll enjoy that later. I'm used to eating small meals. Thank you so much for your kindness." They sipped tea in silence before Kate surprised Lanae.

"Now, I want you to tell me about your Sage. Isn't that his name? The fellow who carried me like Rhett carried Scarlett?"

Lanae wondered if her cheeks reached the color scarlet. "Yes, his name is Sage. I haven't known him very long but I consider him almost as dear to me in the short time I have known him as your Ted was to you."

"Tell me why you say that. I'm all ears, and I have the rest of my life to listen to someone else in love."

Lanae's hand shook. The tea scalded her lips so she set it back in the saucer. "In love?"

"I can feel these things." Kate gave a soft chuckle. "Tell me all about him."

Lanae did. How they met because of the vanity ad. Lezlie and Jaxson. His acreage. His horses. She even mentioned the pictures of Becca, and was surprised when she peeked at her watch to see that more than an hour had passed.

The women cleared and washed the dishes together, setting them in a drain Kate pulled from underneath the sink.

Lanae shrugged into her coat and after pulling on her gloves, was taken aback when Kate hugged her.

"You'll never know how much your visit means to me."

Lanae hugged her back. "I believe when the Lord brings another person to mind, and that person doesn't leave your thoughts, we're supposed to do something more than pray."

"Here, let me turn the light on for you," Kate said before opening the door. "And one more thing. You and Sage have a uniquely personal connection. You've each survived a spouse's death. You've both grieved. You've both been lonely. God will use that."

She and Sage were both used to sleeping single in a double bed, as the old country song went.

14

Life is full of second chances.

Lanae had a grand time greeting new and familiar customers and watching merchandise fly out the door in specialty bags. The Christmas rush was in full swing, and she thrived on the constant activity. To the delight of the *Frivolities* co-owners, men were venturing in to purchase gifts for their women. All thanks to word of mouth, rather than an actual "men's corner." Yet.

She'd had to push thoughts of Sage and her feelings for him to the back of her mind. They appeared just before sleep took her, but her mind succumbed to her body's need for rest.

She was convinced the extra activity might be too much for Geneva. Combined with the onset of colder, wetter weather, her sister's arthritis was acting up. Moselle had made it a point to be around for the coffee brewing and mixing moments, much to Geneva's disgust when her hands didn't do what her mind wanted them to.

"Physical limitations are part of life," Lanae reminded Geneva.

Rainn appeared to fall more in love with Geneva every time Lanae saw them together. She sighed with the beauty, the blessing, of her sister's relationship.

Saturday morning found Lanae thankful Beth Phillips was the extra help *Frivolities* needed. During a lull, Lanae called Lezlie.

"Hey, Lezlie. I'm taking a break, and I thought of your family. Holidays can be tough times when it comes to family memories, and I know it isn't really my business—"

"If you're talking about the letters and what Dad told us the other night," Lezlie interrupted, "Lanae, Jaxson and I owe you. Dad could have taken the Tippin family secret to his grave."

"I suggest, since the secret is now out, I want you and Jaxson to forgive your father. He must have had his reasons for holding back about the way your grandfather died."

"I know, and that's a done deal. I have forgiven him. As soon as I had the chance, I Googled the Earl Tippin and Ted Tippin names, but even when I specified Platteville and Lincoln, I only came up with white pages from telephone directories."

"Same thing happened to me. So many people have cell phones these days. But back to your dad. Think about how the tragedy must have haunted umpteen July Fourth holidays for your father."

"That's not it, Lanae." Lezlie's voice trembled.

Lanae reached out with a mental hug.

"My mother died on Christmas Eve."

Later, Lanae had no idea how she had ended the call. She dealt with people throughout the day, and even did some accounting, but she'd been preoccupied with Sage and what his family had dealt with over the years. Reading between the lines, Kate's letters inferred Ted had been physically hurt somehow.

Stirred by the passion of what was left unsaid, that night Lanae made another call. "Hi. I never did see your new saddle. Would you mind if I drive down and have a look?"

"When are you thinking?" Sage sounded preoccupied.

"Tomorrow after church, OK?"

"Sounds good. I made a pot of chili this afternoon, and it's always better the second day. I'll wait for you."

****

On Sunday, the precipitation started with flurries that looked like floating feathers in various sizes. Then it got heavier and clung to the wet, still-green-in-spots grass of a nearby golf course. The north wind picked up and by the time Lanae pulled into Sage's driveway, the moisture had started to freeze. Some of those ice balls collected like foam beads, circling in the corners around Sage's front door.

"Bad weather report just came on," Sage greeted her. "The storm hit Kansas fast and furious a couple hours ago. Ice, then snow. Looks like we're going to get blasted. Snow is blowing down from Canada, so we'll get hit from two directions."

"How serious is it?"

"Serious enough that you won't be going anywhere soon, and a smart woman would have stayed home. White-out conditions. Patrol says to stay off the roads."

"Good thing you made a pot of chili then. I baked bread. And for your information, I thrive on a grand winter storm as much as I love the rain. I don't think that makes me dumb."

"Seems like all I do is apologize to you, Lanae. Don't most men bark when people they care about put themselves in danger?"

He cares!

But, I haven't been alone with a man since Keith. Storm or no.

****

I haven't been alone with a woman since Becca.

Sage took a seat at the table next to Lanae, inhaling the spicy scent of chili peppers. As she bowed her head, the door burst open.

"Oh, Dad, it's bad out there!"

"What in the world? Doesn't anybody listen to weather reports?"

Lezlie whipped off her coat and hung it on the coat tree. "You've told me before, Dad, that storms have to begin and end somewhere."

For emphasis, ice pinged against the windows. Lanae got up from her seat to take a closer look.

"Way cool." Jaxson slung his coat toward the rack, but it slid to the floor. "We only had flurries at our house, Grandpa."

"It didn't turn to sleet until I hit Highway 2. By then I was much closer to your house than mine," Lezlie finished.

"OK, come in where it's warm. I see Lanae's already set a couple more places. Jax, wanna get some weather on the TV—after you hang up your coat—so we know what's going on here."

"Sure, Grandpa."

The women finished setting the table, and they had taken their seats by the time Jaxson bounded back up the stairs.

"The worst of it angles through Kansas, tips Missouri, and heads into Iowa," Jaxson announced in a deep reporter's exaggerated voice. He swung a leg over the chair back instead of pulling out the chair and slid onto the seat.

"We're on the edge then," Sage said, relieved.

"It's bad enough the highway patrol says don't go anywhere. That's so cool. School's closed for tomorrow already."

"Thanks for checking. Let's eat."

Lanae put a hand on Sage's arm when he scooped up a spoon of chili. "Do you mind if I pray?"

He was so out of the habit.

Lezlie met his gaze before bowing her head.

Sage rested his spoon against the rim of his soup bowl and closed his eyes.

Lanae's breathy alto filled the room. and the hollows of his heart hurt when instead of what he expected, she sang, "The Lord's Prayer."

Silence met her amen.

Jaxson broke it with, "I'm hungry. That was pretty sweet."

"Lanae, that was beautiful. Thank you. I read Matthew six not too long ago. You know, it's called The Lord's prayer, but it really is an example Jesus gave His Disciples as to how we ought to pray." Lezlie turned to her father. "Dad, isn't it time you got out your Bible?"

Sage didn't answer his daughter. He bent his head and blinked the tear off his eyelash into his chili. He'd lost his appetite. The spices clogged his throat. The red chili beans felt like a lump in his stomach, but he managed to eat so nobody had reason to make a big deal out of it.

The foursome made short work of cleaning up the kitchen. Sage didn't join in the light banter. His thoughts were on the weather.

Lezlie planted her feet, hands propped on her hips, and looked her father in the eye. "Dad, I'm going to dig Mom's Bible out of the cedar chest. It's still there, isn't it?"

The Book where Becca had made the notation: *We read to know we're not alone.*

He gave Lezlie a nod and looked at the clock. Three o'clock in the afternoon, and it was as dark as though the sun had already set.

"I'm going out for firewood and to check on the horses," Sage announced. It was a wet, slippery adventure that had him panting by the time he stacked more wood next to the walk-out slider downstairs. He opened the door with enough force to make Jaxson jump. Sage heard the remote drop onto the coffee table.

"Jax! Get your mom's keys and come help me. There's a coating of ice on the windshields already. Ask Lanae for her car keys, too, please. We're going to put the vehicles in the barn so we don't have to scrape this mess again later. The sky is trying to decide if it's spitting ice or blowing snow."

The vehicles' defrost functions helped melt the thin layer of ice off the sedan and SUV while Sage and his grandson scraped windows without many words. On their return walk to the house, two inches of powdery snow covered the slick rock of the driveway.

"Grandpa, I think I forgot something back there. I'll see you in a few."

Sage jostled Jaxson's stocking cap, exposing an ear until it hunkered over the opposite eye. "I understand.

If I didn't feel this humidity deep in my bones, I'd stay out and play myself."

The action brought back a reminder of Jaxson at age four. Sage pulled him close, tucked the cap back in place, and started to sing.

"I love you a bushel and a peck. A bushel and a peck and a hug around the neck."

Jaxson struggled to get loose. "Come on, Gramps. I'm not a kid anymore."

"Well, I don't tell you enough how much I love you, and I sure hope we continue to offer hugs to each other until one of us dies."

"Gross. I love you, too. But let me go, already." Jaxson protested with a laugh.

Sage was half chuckling and half singing when he stomped his boots off inside the garage door. Maybe it was good, this company thing. He thumped the hood of his truck, thankful he'd squeezed it inside away from the storm. Unused to women in his home, he stopped a moment to collect himself and figure out what to do next.

When he opened the door, he saw Lezlie huddled in the recliner underneath a frayed blanket, looking so much like Becca that any words he could have formed froze in his throat.

****

Lanae looked up from the game drawer Lezlie had directed her to when Sage hustled through the door. He stood with mouth agape while the frigid air drafted across the room. A loose card from a box drifted to the floor next to her feet.

What in the world? Sage stared at Lezlie like he

was looking at a ghost.

"Hey, Dad, where's Jax—"

Sage grunted as Jaxson barreled through the door, knocking Sage forward. He gained his balance and came out of his daze enough to shrug off his coat.

"Look what I found in the barn. I've heard you guys talk about these letters. But hey, I didn't pay much attention. What were they doing in the trash bucket in the barn, Grandpa?"

Sage scowled instead of answering. He stormed into the kitchen where he searched the bottom of the coffee carafe as though it held answers to the world's peace problems.

"Jax, I love you!" Lezlie grabbed the discarded packet of letters from her son. "Dad, I'm not going to believe you threw them away on purpose. Lanae, have you read all of them?"

Lanae's heart picked up its pace. With a sliding glance directed at Sage, she answered, "I have to confess, that yes, I went through them."

"Dad, quit pretending these letters don't exist, and get in here. We're reading them. Thanks, Jaxson, for bringing them in."

"Sure. Probably all mushy kisses and stuff. I'm starved."

Lanae found a seat and sat back to watch Lezlie run the show, getting a kick out of the way Sage still frowned. But to his credit, he let Lezlie take charge. She looked at the posted dates without changing the order, and handed every other letter to her father.

He sat down on the couch next to Lanae.

"Dad, I want you to know how important this is to me, getting a glimpse of an uncle I've never known about. I can't emphasize enough how when both

Jaxson and I were kids...well, like I said before, it was embarrassing not knowing the names in our family tree for school projects." Lezlie tucked the letters in her hand and took the rest to her father. She hugged him. "I couldn't tell you the way I felt, but it was like I was adopted or something—"

"Yeah, Ma. I felt the same, but I was too embarrassed to tell you. It's huge that I always have to put 'unknown' for my father." Jaxson headed downstairs.

"This is not the time." Lezlie stepped back and looked at her son.

He slumped his shoulders and instead of taking the stairs, draped his lanky arms over the banister rail as though he needed the iron to hold him upright.

Lanae found it quite dramatic, this interesting family situation, for mother and son to discover they had the same thoughts. Yet, they hadn't gone to the necessary lengths to discover ancestral answers. Instead, they'd accepted poor grades for incomplete school assignments.

Lezlie resumed her seat, carefully unfolded the top letter, and started to read aloud.

While Lezlie was reading, Sage stared off with a glazed-over expression that told Lanae he wasn't seeing or listening to a thing.

She followed Sage's gaze out the window and gasped. Snow no longer fell. The outdoor world was bright white. A flock of cardinals, maybe a dozen, perched in a bush. Never in her life had she seen so many male cardinals so close together. The females wore fluffed feathers against the cold, making their shape rounder and softer looking than the males.

But why was Sage enthralled by the sight?

Lanae watched the birds, mesmerized. The brilliant scarlet males against the pure snow, perched vivid in the ethereal backdrop, brought to mind the shed blood of Jesus. Once a soul believed, Christ saw a saint as pure, white as snow. Without sin.

Lezlie interrupted. "What's going on? You're both not here in this room, by the looks on your faces."

"Sorry." Lanae didn't make eye contact with Lezlie and lost track of which letter had just been read. "Guess I zoned out. I get choked up over Kate's passionate, unfulfilled secret longings."

"Lanae, what is your secret longing?" Lezlie asked, her words dropping like rocks. The young woman had no problem asking difficult questions.

"That can be a loaded question and differs according to where I am in my life." Lanae answered, not meeting Sage's eyes.

"Right now," Sage said, touching her shoulder.

"Right now, I'm envious of your home. I wish for a home just like it. I miss the country so." She jumped up. "And I shouldn't. I know. I should be content where I am, thankful to be disease free. I think I need something to drink. May I?"

"There's cranberry juice, apple cider, and cocoa makings in there." Sage said easily. "Help yourself."

On her way to the kitchen, she caught sight of the telephone, which reminded her to check in with Geneva, considering the weather.

After using her cell to leave a message for her sister, hot cranberry juice in hand, Lanae stood at the counter. She listened as Sage tried to read Kate's written words without inflection.

Lord, what is he feeling? Thinking? Do the words make him yearn for Becca, bring back his own loss? Does he wonder about Ted and what happened to him? Where he went?

They were so involved with reading the letters that Jaxson startled them all when he burst through the front door. Lanae hadn't even realized he'd gone out again, probably through the walk-out downstairs.

"Wow, guys. It's crazy out there! There's a glaze on top of the snow so every step I took crunched and broke like I was on ice breaking on the water. Way cool. Check this out." Jaxson turned his back, and dragged a huge pine bough, dripping snow, through the front door.

Sage hurried to slam out the blast of icy air.

Jaxson kept right on talking. "The ice broke this off and when I saw it, I grabbed it. Grandpa, I've never seen a Christmas tree in your place. We've got one now."

Sage ignored the commotion and trounced down the hall, mumbling what sounded like, "sewing supplies."

"I'll find something to stand this branch in," Jax said, on his way to the garage. "I've got this tree business under control."

Lezlie shrugged and set aside the letters. "Guess we'll finish these later. I'll pop some corn for stringing."

Lanae turned on the radio, and a Christmas-carol medley filled the air. An hour later, the adults were scrunched tight on the couch, and Jaxson sat in the recliner. They remained in silence with the lights off, hot chocolate in hand.

The "tree" looked all right where it listed some from its foundation of sand in a gallon can covered with foil. Sage had surprised them all when he brought out a jar of colored buttons, reminding Lanae of Geneva's vast collection. Using needles and thread, they had strung strands of buttons as well as popcorn, and Lezlie created a garland of colored paper clips. Jaxson covered star-shaped cardboard in foil to top it all off. The tree looked colorful with their efforts.

Lanae wondered. This family owned no ornaments. Perhaps they made them each year, or maybe, with the death of Becca, they simply celebrated at Lezlie's house, and Sage didn't bother with a tree at his own home. Somehow, that seemed so sad.

Later, the snow outside the windows and the fire inside made it feel as though they were wrapped in a cocoon of warmth. Lanae snuggled in a little closer to Sage, where they shared the couch with Lezlie. She didn't want to be anywhere else in the world.

Jaxson gulped the last of his hot chocolate, angled out of the big leather recliner, and announced he'd see them in the morning.

"You'll be OK down there with the blanket and couch pillow?" Sage asked.

"No problem. I'll catch a late show, but I'll keep it low, so you don't hear the TV."

They all stood. Sage grabbed the mugs and took them to the sink. Lezlie walked to the top of the stairs to give Jaxson a hug.

Lanae called after them. "The tree was a nice gift to your grandfather, Jaxson, and I'll cherish the memory."

He blushed and disappeared.

Lezlie yawned before addressing Lanae. "Are you sure you don't mind sharing a room? I could sleep out here."

"No problem at all."

Lezlie went to the kitchen and hugged Sage. "I'm going to turn in, too, Dad. Goodnight."

Sage kissed her on the cheek and waited until the bathroom door closed before he resumed his seat on the couch. He grabbed the cover Lezlie had abandoned and motioned for Lenae to join him.

She cozied in next to him, where she'd been earlier, and leaned her head on his shoulder.

He clasped her hand after she smoothed the frayed blanket over their legs, and kissed the top of her head. "What was your comment earlier about being discontent?"

"I miss the ranch. I was thinking about horses and was reminded that West Nile virus had just come into the open. But we never had a vaccine as part of our routine care. Somehow, I thought I'd stay there until I died. That last morning when I gave up my life out west, I remember rising slowly from the breakfast table and hesitating a moment before opening the door. A storm raged in my heart and had been gathering speed and depth until it erupted into a flood of tears. I wondered if I was making a mistake after all. But living in the middle of nowhere, alone, I knew deep inside I was meant to start over, to move to Platteville and begin a new season of my life with Geneva and *Frivolities*."

Sage stared at the flames in the fireplace. "Yeah, I know about new beginnings. I couldn't concentrate on my job in Lincoln after I lost Becca and moved around some. When I ran across this acreage, I knew it was the place for me to start over. Can't believe I've been here five years already."

"I was thankful Keith and I had had no children to witness my humiliation and defeat. The finality of the sale delivered a stinging blow. How often I prided myself on my skills as a rancher after he was killed, taking care of the land for God. Now it's difficult to believe the way I kept going it alone as long as I did. God was with me, I know. Keith and I had worked so hard, I couldn't just give up."

"You grieved for the land the way I did when I sold our home. I couldn't live there after Becca died. I slept on the couch. Not this one. Couldn't even go in the bedroom we'd shared. Lezlie and Becca's sister packed up her things."

At the mention of his dead wife, Sage released Lanae's hand from where he had held it close to his side. Was he hiding their connection from Becca's prying, photograph eyes?

Lanae felt the absence of his touch, brief as it had been. Sage had kept his distance all night, she suspected for the sake of Lezlie and Jaxson.

She continued her story. "Later, driving away, I felt a vast emptiness every bit as bone-deep as the one I had experienced after losing Keith to the accident. The ranch had become like a living thing to me, maybe even an idol the Bible talks about. Certainly there were times I put it before my relationship with the Lord. Just imagine, Sage, if you had to leave your land and move to the city."

"I'd be lost. And angry. I don't want to imagine facing a concrete jungle again on a daily basis. Or the idea of ever punching a time clock again."

"Well, it was an adjustment all right, but I really didn't have the chance to miss the beautiful land, the huge sky, the expanse of the horizon..." Agitated with herself, she scooted forward and put the sewing things back in order. "I got sick and probably was sick long before I left western Nebraska."

She felt Sage stiffen and pull back. "I don't think I could do it again, go through that pain."

"You've been sick?"

"Not me. But I've watched someone sick for a long time. That feeling of helplessness left me raw."

Lanae continued as though he hadn't commented. "It was such a shock, to be diagnosed with hepatitis C." Lanae placed several western and horse magazines into a stack and then shuffled the cards in the game box. "Until I researched the disease, I was convinced that long ago I caused it when I did something stupid." She held the cards and looked over her shoulder to gauge his reaction. "I had a one-night stand when I was grieving, and missing Keith so much I wasn't in my right mind. I figured the virus was my punishment. But as it turned out, sexual contact is a rare way to contract the disease."

"So how'd you get it then?"

"It had to have been during that old surgery. Anyway, eighty percent of the people infected have no noticeable signs or symptoms, but we do experience emotional expressions like depression and panic attacks. I thought I was too excited and working too hard getting *Frivolities* under way."

He looked like he wanted to be anywhere else in the world.

"As soon as I realized my life could be terminal, I got down on myself for feeling sorry and dissatisfied. I decided to live, no matter what the circumstance. I got so excited, inspired, even consumed, by the business of *Frivolities*. I crocheted like a mad woman. Each day I looked for the presence of God in the smallest things. My life is so rich with Eric and Moselle, Rainn and Mia.

And of course, Geneva. I don't know if I would have made it without her."

Sage took the cards from where she'd dropped them on the coffee table and counted out thirty into two stacks. He hesitated, staring hard at the cards. "I couldn't deal with it ever again. And I refuse to take the chance of facing another loved one's terminal illness—"

"Now wait," Lanae interrupted, "we don't know what God has planned for anyone's life."

His face turned into an expressionless mask, as though an invisible hand had wiped it clear. He turned the card on top of his pile face-up, evened the stack in a precise rectangle.

She turned up a number one and took the five cards Sage dealt her. But instead of continuing her turn, she laid the cards down and reached for his hand. "Sage, I don't care for these disagreeable feelings between us. Would you pray with me?"

He folded his cards in one hand and clasped her fingers, released a heavy sigh, and nodded.

"Dear heavenly Father. Thank You for the shelter we've had against the storm. Thank You for Sage and the safety of his home. I praise You for renewing anxious hearts, replacing those human emotions with a peace that surpasses understanding. Please show Kate a special grace at this moment, and if Ted is still around, only You know where he is. Now I ask that You guide us through the rest of this night."

Sage squeezed her hand, inhaled, and blew it out on a heavy sigh.

She reached for one of Kate's letters and handed it to Sage. "You didn't read them all. I want to hear this in your voice."

He slapped his cards on the table, avoided her eyes, and snatched the letter. He began to read.

July 19, 1960
The middle of the night

Dear, Dearest Theodore,
I finally drove to your place and met your mother. She is grieving as much for you as she is for your father.
For the sake of my own health, I fear I need to quit writing you these letters.
Maybe I am growing up. I braved up enough courage to tell my father I'm going to get a job in Omaha. One of the reasons is that I can't be here in this room where I have loved you and been held in your arms through more dreams than I care to begin to count.
Your mother must have given up on your coming back.
She returned to me the photograph I gave you. You know the one, where I'm sitting on our cellar door, in my jumpsuit shorts. You teased me about my pretty legs and pin-curled hair.
I'll love you forever, my one and only true love.

Good-bye,
Katherine

When he stopped reading, Sage kept his eyes lowered. He carefully folded the letter, set it down almost reverently, and leaned back. The only sound in the room came from the wind whining outside.

Lanae couldn't speak yet. Her body shook inside, and silent tears slid down her cheeks, the same way she had wept when she'd first read the poignant missive. This time, hearing the words through Sage, sent a thrill down her spine. The timbre of his voice held the quality of cooing doves. Tension eased, the way a massage therapist removed knots from tired muscles, yet her whole being tingled.

She tried to look into his eyes, but he kept them diverted. Her hope of any elaboration vanished.

Sage was leaving something out.

He knew more than he let on.

Lanae was more determined than ever to stick this out until the full story of Katherine and Ted was in the open. For everyone involved. Kate. Lezlie and Jaxson. Sage. Even Ted Tippin, wherever he may be.

Sage swallowed loud enough for Lanae to hear the gulp. "I can't get over it. Kate Rawlins, whom I've heard called the certifiable Platteville windbag, is Katherine."

"And her Teddy. Katherine, or Kate's Theodore, is Ted Tippin. Your uncle."

"Yep. But my Uncle Ted is gone. Who knows where. Who knows if he's dead or alive? And whatever happened the day he disappeared is in the past. I don't believe the past really matters if it takes joy from life in the here and now."

"What joy, Sage? Where is your joy? You're always so serious. Remember when you were young and you laughed, just so full of life, for no other reason than because you could? Because you were alive?"

"Not really. I was young a long time ago."

Lanae snorted. "My sister can assure you we're only as young as we feel. Love turned Geneva into a teenager again. And I'm sorry you feel so old. Back to past and present. Don't you want to give Jaxson memories of the present rather than keep past secrets? This pine tree tonight meant a lot to him. He and Lezlie deserve to have the best of you."

"Once upon a time, I had the best of Uncle Ted. My mom called him a blessing."

"We all need to be happy for the blessings, even if they are memories. We should be thankful for the people God puts in our lives. Past and present and future." Lanae stood with her eyes on Becca's image. "We have to move on, Sage. Can you continue this way? Does her memory keep you warm at night?"

She folded the blanket with precision. "I'd like nothing more than a chance to love you, but there's someone between us."

Sage drew in a breath, as though he was going to speak. He didn't.

"I'm going to bed." She tossed the blanket into the corner of the recliner, where it landed in a tented heap, mocking her meticulous folds.

Lanae felt his gaze burning into her while she crossed the room. The knowledge came as sure as horses have tails. Dare she? She did. Lanae swung around and caught Sage watching her.

He studied her with troubled, puzzled eyes. "I don't understand how you think you can love me. I'm not looking for love. I'm damaged. I don't think I believe in God anymore. And, I imagine you're right when you say I still love my wife."

"Sage, I was in love with Keith. But our love was in the past. At some point I left him there and began to live for the future. I gave up being in love with Keith. Now I can love the memory of him and what we had while he was here."

Sage got up and ambled close, never breaking their eye contact.

She sucked in a breath. And held it.

"OK, I confess. I was comfortable loving Becca. But what I feel for you..." He shook his head as though to clear it. "Sometimes I don't like it. I get all unfocused in the head. Happy and goofy, yet aching, almost to the point of hurting. Never think I don't want you."

An implosion of reaction followed his words. Lanae was hot and cold, excited and numb, all at the same time. She could only stare back at him.

"I may want you, sweet Lanae, but to me it feels like a betrayal of Becca's love."

She gasped, blurted, "Why in the world is it so hard for you to accept today, and what God has in store for our pleasure? Put yesterday away." She spun on her heel, and refused to believe what he had just said. A person in the grave cannot keep another one warm at night.

In the guest room where Lezlie slept, Lanae opened her thoughts to God.

This is so typical, and I am so sorry, Lord, for waiting until tonight to talk to You. You are the Master of the Universe, yet You wait for some human like me to call on You. I wait until the day's activity is over, when I needed Your strength to get me through, before I consciously remember You planned my day.

But I'm as confused as Sage seems to be. You know where my heart is right now. You know my longings. You also know my discontent, and I ask for help to get beyond that. Please help me know where I'm supposed to go from here.

15

Monday morning found Sage restless. He wasn't used to having people in the house, so he hadn't slept much. Before he lumbered out of bed, he planned how he'd hook up the blade on his truck and clear the drive. Jax could help get the women's vehicles out of the barn.

Women. One woman, rather, had weighed on his mind throughout the night. He hadn't slept much. The sight of Lanae in the hallway had been ever present behind his eyelids. More accurate, his reactions to Lanae had kept him awake until two-thirty.

All sorts of emotions galloped through him upon rising. He valued Lanae's friendship, but Sage refused to believe he could consider her as more than a friend. But she was at the forefront of his mind more and more as days passed. He was drawn to her outlook on life as well as the man-woman attraction.

The God issue played a part as well. He slung the heavy blanket off his chest. He punched the king-sized pillow at his side.

He might just as well acknowledge Him.

"God, I know you're there for some people. How can I ever forget the way I prayed for You to spare Becca? I begged for You to perform a miracle in her cancer-swollen body. I bargained, and I lost. You took her, anyway." Sage ground his teeth. He jerked his eyes open and kicked aside the bed covers.

It'd never work with Lanae. She had a child-like trust. She came across as though she lived in a black and white world. She wanted answers about Uncle Ted. She even believed Ted was out there somewhere, just the way Katherine had turned out to be Kate.

I need to keep what happened in the past secret.

And like a flash, ancient words from his past came to mind. *He knows the secrets of the heart.*

Sage recognized the words from Psalm 44, and a sharp pain pierced his heart. God knows. Then his eyes focused on Becca's picture, where she looked out and greeted him each morning.

"I'd like to think of you at Lanae's age, full of life and energy. But I only remember how you suffered with a disease that stole my life as much as it took yours, and how God let you suffer." He turned his whole body to face the photo on his night table and stared into the brown eyes. He looked at the mouth that didn't answer back, reached out to run his thumb over the inanimate object. A new concept shot through him as he waited in the quiet room.

Becca didn't "talk" back like he usually imagined. Her voice was absent from his skull.

It hit him hard enough to bring tears to his eyes.

Sage couldn't hear Becca's voice any longer. What he heard instead, zinging through his head, was Lanae's lilting laughter.

Actually, it'd been some time since he'd gone through the rooms in turn, telling Becca about his day.

By the time he readied himself, he realized he looked forward to saying good morning to everyone, especially a certain spunky woman.

He passed Jax snoring on the couch. He quietly

ascended the stairs. He thought he heard one of the gals running water in the guest bathroom, but the house was silent again, so he went on to the great room. Sage cleared ashes from the grate in the fireplace and put on another log.

When he stood, Becca smiled from her mantle photo. He took the picture down, ran a finger over the top of the frame to remove any dust, then held her close to his heart.

Becca had looked back at him from within the frames of her various pictures since he'd moved into the ranch house, always with a trusting look in her brown eyes that said she thought he hung the moon.

But his moon had dropped right out of the sky when she died.

It was time to put her away.

His shoulders soon heaved with the magnitude of his tears.

****

Don't save things for a special occasion. I'm alive today. It's a special occasion right now.

Sleep hovered like a flowing black cape just beyond her reach. Throughout the night, Lanae opened her eyes and turned to the bedside clock, noting every hour. Always, she took care not to disturb Lezlie. As a result, she woke with a blinding headache.

When she ambled down the hall, she inhaled the fresh brewed coffee that must have been on a timer. She'd heard no one in the kitchen. She jolted at seeing Sage in the great room. The sight before her stabbed her heart.

Sage, body jerking with silent sobs, cradled Becca's framed picture.

Lanae's mind went blank. She stumbled, caught herself before she could make a sound, and retreated without turning around. She tiptoed backwards down the hall.

The vision of Sage in such obvious agony burned into her brain like a searing branding iron.

Lanae's tears froze within her. Hopelessness slammed deep to the core of her being. She had to get out of there as soon as she could. She couldn't face Sage alone yet. Lanae returned to the guestroom and feigned sleep. Her heart hurt too badly to form a prayer.

Through her numbness, she listened to Lezlie's movements as she rose and finished in the bathroom.

She heard Jaxson tromp up the stairs and announce his usual hunger. Muffled laughter and the sounds of their voices came from far away as they shared breakfast.

She drifted off, and woke up to her own rudeness, cowardice even, when she heard Sage telling Lezlie and Jaxson good-bye.

Lanae yanked off the tufted blue coverlet and speedily dressed. She scurried through the great room and called out the front door, "Hey, Jax, thanks for bringing those letters in from the barn." She rubbed her arms and stomped her stocking-clad feet to ward off the chill.

"No problem." He stood on the porch with his mother.

"Well, they're important."

Lezlie nodded at her comment.

Sage glared.

"Those letters are so back-before-I-was-born." Jaxson grinned when he made the remark.

"Well, you're a thoughtful young man. The Christmas tree is special." She turned to Lezlie. "What are your plans for Christmas?"

"Hasn't Dad told you? We always go somewhere warm. Florida this year, but Dad's thinking it might be a good place to check out real estate."

Hadn't she had enough shocks for one morning? She froze in place.

The Diamond family walked out to the car together.

Lanae stood inside the door and listened.

"Love you, son," Sage told Jaxson as he shut the passenger door of the SUV.

"And God loves you, Dad," Lezlie told Sage when he went around to the driver's side. Something secret was behind the words.

Lanae wished she was close enough to see their expressions.

When they hugged again, Lanae was able to pry up her feet. She spied her sedan parked behind Lezlie's.

She'd stay long enough for coffee, which she needed for the drive back. "Dill-witted," she told herself. Then she laughed without humor. "You do like dill pickles, but dull-witted, don't you mean?" She needed coffee, and poured a cup before slipping into her shoes. Lanae drank it while leaning against the counter. She purposely ignored looking toward the fireplace and the picture on the mantle.

Had loving Sage ever been in God's plan for her?

Sage must have gone out to the barn, because he didn't return to the house. She was half finished with a

171

second cup of coffee before she decided it might be best to leave without talking to him.

She dug a notepad out of her purse and scrawled a simple thank-you. She found her purse, shoved her arms into her coat, and left.

Traffic was close to nonexistent when she hit the road, and when vehicles moved, they crawled. She was glad, because her mind was everywhere but on her driving. When she came upon Western Row she decided to stop.

How crazy it all was. Lanae had used the excuse of looking at Sage's new saddle to go see him, but the storm and then the letter business had intervened. She had yet to lay her eyes on the new saddle.

Now, after seeing him weep over Becca's picture, she doubted she'd ever see the leather in question.

Sage was an enigma. What made him tick?

When she first met him, Lanae had considered him even-keeled, almost too peaceful, an unemotional observer.

After witnessing his weeping breakdown, he certainly contradicted that impression. So maybe Sage appeared easy going when it involved anyone else but Becca.

Lanae was impressed walking into Western Row. The shops were different, but connected. She wandered through the displays of local artists' work, noticed the difference between a connection with nature and the froufrou fun decorative items of *Frivolities*. Instead of vanilla and spice, these shops smelled of leather. Necessary and unnecessary western apparel came next, where she was drawn to a pair of boots dyed in mauve and turquoise.

"Let me know if I can help you find your size."

Lanae turned to greet the speaker. A lovely, statuesque woman with black hair and stunning amber eyes came to her direction from the farrier end of the row of shops. She brought with her the scent of leather.

"Are you the saddle maker?"

"Lorinda Watts." She gave Lanae a closer look while extending her hand. "Sorry, my hands are so rough."

"No problem. Mine were like that when I lived on the ranch. I'm Lanae Petersen from Platteville."

"Oh! You bought Sage Diamond's vanity?"

Should she be jealous of Lorinda? She tossed away the idea. She couldn't help but wonder about his and another woman's friendship. Sage was obviously self-sufficient, but had he ever turned to Lorinda Watts for more?

"Forgive me for being so forward, but after meeting you, Lanae, I think Sage might finally admit he can't go on living in the past."

"Thanks for your vote of confidence, but I doubt he's ready to take a risk on me."

"OK, change of subject. Is there anything I can help you find?"

"I'd like to see one of your saddles, or anything else you've made."

Lanae kept her eyes peeled for the aesthetics of the displays as she followed Lorinda. Then she kind of let her mind wander while Lorinda explained her leather working tools and stains.

She tuned back in when Lorinda said, "Similar to the one I did for Sage...well, look who's here..."

Lanae could count the number of times she'd been around Sage on her fingers, but each time she looked him in the face, or heard his voice, she reacted like it was the first. It wasn't just the unique blue of his eyes, or his slow manner of speech, but the whole package of outdoor breadth and solidity.

Gooseflesh shivered over her skin as though he had caressed her with an invisible touch. "I can't believe you're here."

His gaze locked on hers. "Fine way to say good-bye, by leaving a note."

Lorinda turned from Sage to Lanae, wide-eyed and grinning from ear to ear.

"It's not how it sounds," Lanae attempted to explain. "I got snowed in—"

"Along with Lezlie and Jax," Sage added.

"You left without seeing my saddle."

"So you followed me?"

"Not really. Yeah. Kinda, I guess. The roads are still dangerous, so I wanted to make sure you got home with no problems. Then I saw your car here, and well, here we both are."

He would have followed her to Platteville? After catching him weeping earlier that morning, she was more thrilled by his protective care than she wanted to admit.

Lanae decided they didn't need a third person taking it all in. "Lorinda, it was great meeting you. Come on up to *Frivolities*, and I'll treat you to some of my sister's coffee."

"Hey, I've been meaning to. Word's out about your cheesecake, so you can count on a visit from me."

Sage tipped his hat, not saying a word to Lorinda, and latched onto Lanae's elbow as though he feared she'd take flight. Outside, he pulled his collar up to protect his neck against a blast of arctic air.

Lanae slunk down into the warmth of her

crocheted scarf, looking at him expectantly.

"I haven't been honest with you. There's another letter, one separate from the ones you found. It's time I showed it to someone." He spoke gruffly.

She hesitated. The flashing image of him wrapped around Becca's picture conflicted with his opening up to her now. But then she was here in the flesh, and his wife was gone.

"Would you mind coming back? Have lunch with me at the house?" He looked so vulnerable, needy even.

"Sure. Let me give Geneva a buzz so she knows where I am," she said, as she dug for her cell phone. "Let's go then. It's freezing out here."

Back at Sage's home, the smell and warmth of burning firewood welcomed her.

Sage took her coat, hands lingering as though he wanted to warm her up with all his movements. "Let's go in by the fire."

She flashed him a smile. *I wouldn't want to be anywhere else.*

"When I was packing up to move to the acreage..." Sage reached for a heavy blanket with a Native American design in primary colors, covered their legs where they nearly touched on the couch. "I found a letter folded up in the support board for the mirror."

Lanae was glad he sat near but confused enough she couldn't quite relax.

"It's from my Uncle Ted, written to his mother."

"That'd be your grandmother, Juanita?"

"Right. My grandmother must have finally given up, realized her son was never coming back, and hid the letters Katherine had written. My mom got the dresser after Grandma died. She may not have even known about the letters."

"But you've known about this one?"

He gave her a shame-faced nod. "I had never heard of Katherine before you found the others, and to find out she loved my uncle and had met my grandmother, well, that was a lot to put together."

He picked up an unfolded, hand-written sheet of paper with fragile fold creases. "I can't remember if I told you my grandfather Earl was an unpleasant sort. To put it mildly. World War II changed the man, turned him into an angry, abusive drunk."

"I thought we knew enough about one another that you could have trusted me with this letter earlier."

"Didn't you ever have a secret?"

Since he was confessing, she considered telling Sage more about her one-night stand.

Now wasn't the time. Maybe she didn't trust him enough.

"Uncle Ted had taken enough. He resolved to take no more beatings and at the same time protect the women in the family. In the heat of the moment, my uncle hit his own father four times with a broken ax handle. I tried to spare my daughter and grandson from the details of my grandfather's cruelty. However, they need to know about their uncle, so I guess it's time the whole story comes out in the open."

"Katherine surfaced. There's a chance your uncle is still out there somewhere." Nerve endings skittered throughout her body as Lanae began to read.

Somewhere in Alaska
July 1975

My Dearest Mother,

It's been fifteen years, and I don't know where to begin. You are a wise woman. No doubt you figured out the connection between his death and my disappearance.

Like David in the Psalms, I can finally say I have discovered peace.

God forgives.

Now, I'm asking you to forgive me.

For reasons known only to you, you loved my father.

I hated him.

You told me more times than I can count how much he had changed, that he hadn't always been the way he was with us.

I couldn't stand it anymore. I'm a man. My body healed, but I'd had enough. And I wanted to free you all from his tyranny.

The blows he gave your heart, did they ever heal?

I caused you more hurt, I can only imagine. I so hope you can forgive me.

It was an ugly scene on that Fourth of July. My mind snapped the way the ax handle had snapped after he wrestled it from my hands and slung it against the Old Packard.

I got it away from him and pounded on him to get him to stop hurting us.

I could stop him, that's all I wanted. I never intended to kill him. I didn't know what else to do. So I ran.

My precious mother, I know that we will meet again in the great by and by.

Your only son,

Theodore

P.S. *"My hope is in you all day long,"* Psalm 25:5.

Lanae was thankful for the leather cushion beneath her. Her legs wouldn't have held her had she been standing.

16

Live—because God gave me life.
Soar—because God gives my soul wings.

"Have you heard anything else from him?"

Sage lowered his eyelids. His mouth frowned.

Lanae's heart pinched. She swallowed in reaction to all she saw in his face. Sorrow. Pain. Defeat. Hopelessness. He needed her. Could the Lord use her to lift his heart so he could live the way God wanted him to?

"I have no idea what happened to him. Where he went. This is the only connection to Uncle Ted since that long-ago July Fourth when he disappeared."

"Your poor mother. Were you close to him, Sage?"

"He was my mentor. My role model. Closer to me than my own father."

"Tell me something good you remember about your uncle."

"He loved me."

Lanae waited while he searched his memory.

"I was four, maybe five. I fell down, tore a hole in my britches, and scraped my knee." Sage chuckled.

She loved the play of emotions that softened his face. He shook his head and grinned.

"Ted said, 'come here, and I'll pick you up.' When he knew I got it, that I was already standing up so he couldn't pick me up, he broke up. He had a deep belly laugh, like his whole body was tickled."

"Haven't you ever wondered if Ted is still alive?"

"Of course. As much as I've wanted to try to find him, I've been a coward. I know there's no statute of limitations on murder. If my uncle were found, he'd have to face the law in Nebraska, face the consequences. With no witnesses after all this time, could he claim self defense?" Sage slumped against the back of the sofa, scrubbed both hands over his face.

Lanae leaned in close, circled her hand over his chest. They sat quiet for a few moments before she jerked up. "Sage, I think Kate Rawlins needs to know what happened."

When he drew a breath to speak, she felt the movement in her fingertips.

"The more the merrier. I'll have to tell Lezlie as well. It can't be hidden forever. As for the truth coming out," he scrubbed a weather-beaten hand through his hair and down his face, "I've wondered if I could be in trouble. For aiding and abetting or hiding evidence. Whatever. I pretty much have a tangible confession right here in my possession. I don't know who it's safe to tell."

****

Two hours later, Lanae was on her way home. Again.

A storm raged inside every bit as fierce as the icy snow that had beat against the ranch house the afternoon before.

She had interfered.

Remorse was the only word that came to mind to

describe how she felt after finding out the way Earl Tippin died.

Maybe sorrow.

She'd hurt Sage. And Lezlie and Jaxson.

This was another instance where the past probably needed to stay in the past.

In all of her searching to find the mysterious letter writer and recipient, had she ever prayed about it? If she had, it was no doubt flippant. And she hadn't left the request with Jesus. She'd gone on her own and forced the issue.

At the sight of a soaring eagle, her thoughts were drawn to Isaiah 40. She tried to keep her car on the road as she watched the tips of its wings where it sailed above the river. Its white head reflected gold where the rays of sun hit it just right.

"Lord, forgive my impatience. Help me rest patiently as I gain new strength. Please help Sage rest in You as well, and remove his weariness. Enable him to mount up with wings of eagles."

When she could no longer see the eagle, she blinked to clear her vision. Unsure of what danced above the horizon, she blinked again. But it was indeed there. She was looking at a winter rainbow, dimly ethereal and pastel in the white western sky. Snow glistened in streams of sunlight at the same time. Who would believe it? She knew it was a sundog, the halo effect and bright spots of light radiating, but the rainbow spectacle stole her breath.

"Oh, Lord, You are beyond compare. I'm weary from lack of sleep and convoluted feelings about Sage and where he's coming from. You lift my heart like the wings of an eagle when I'm too weary for words. You place your rainbow symbol of promises kept, right there in the sky for humans to see. Whoever else sees this rainbow, please bless them. And, oh Lord, forgive me for not asking You to find Ted Tippin, if he is meant to be in Sage and Kate's lives again."

She said thanks and amen and turned her car Kate Rawlins' way rather than the alley behind *Frivolities*.

Something in Kate drew Lanae. Maybe she empathized deeper because of the letters she'd read. Or maybe Katherine's loss of Ted brought to mind losing Keith.

After Lanae greeted Kate with a hug, Kate said, "I don't know why you're being so nice to me. I've wasted my life. I'm an embarrassment to God, the way I turned so unhappy and bitter."

Lanae swiped at her empathetic tears that gathered and threatened to spill down her cheeks. "Kate, you're not the only one with regrets. Let's put on some hot water, and I'll do a little confessing of my own."

"I'd like that. Not a confession, but your company over a hot drink. I don't deserve your time." Kate turned on the faucet.

"We all deserve time and a second chance. God forgives us, so we need to forgive ourselves as well as others."

Kate sniffled, and motioned with her hand. "Have a seat at the table, and I'll use the microwave."

Once Kate joined her, Lanae began, "I have something to tell you about your Ted. I'm trying to soak it in myself. It's quite the story."

When Lanae finished explaining the contents of the letter from Alaska, Kate sat pale and shaken. Lanae reasoned it would take some time for Kate to absorb the whole thing. Her Ted, whom Katherine thought had abandoned her, had murdered his own father before disappearing.

"Looks like I definitely need to spend time on my knees. Thank you for becoming a good friend. Now, did you say something about confessing?"

Lanae let the hot cider sit, but cupped her hands around the warmth of the mug. "Who am I to pass judgment on your Ted? I did something stupid on the second anniversary of my husband's death. Out of my head with grief, I railed at God. He never answered when I asked about a zillion times why Keith had been killed."

Just say it. Everyone has a past. "I had a one-night stand over twenty years ago. I drove to a tavern way out in the Sandhills boonies. For years, I buried that night so deep that it was like another woman had done the deed."

Kate placed her warm hand over Lanae's forearm, stroked her twice.

"For a while I was convinced that mistake was how I contracted the hepatitis C virus. I kept the secret. Way down deep I came to realize that I can forgive others because God has forgiven me much. Now He needs to forgive me for wanting something more out of life than I already have."

She blinked and managed a sad smile when Kate gave her arm a squeeze. Lanae continued. "I was a believer at the time, but I got caught in a moment of weakness. The guy had a deep, silky voice and a mustache to match. And that smile drove me wild. Every time he drawled, extra long, 'Ma'aa'am,' he sent me into orbit. Cowboys are my weakness. It's strange, but I can't remember his real name. Every time I recalled that night, fuzzy as it became over the years,

I'd named him Cowboy Sam in my mind."

She'd asked for and received forgiveness a long time ago. But by telling Kate, it helped to sort out the details of what Sage had lived with. She knew it was against God's nature to remember her sin. His grace covered her weakness, and Jesus paid for it. So even though sometimes it felt like her disease was a punishment, logically, Lanae knew it had nothing to do with her past sin but was merely a trial allowed by God to strengthen her faith.

Kate stared down into her coffee then met Lanae's gaze and started to speak. "I was bitter after being jilted, that Teddy left because of me, and now I'm so appalled to discover it was a mistake on my part. Now I regret that I took my misinterpretation out on everyone else. Look at my skewed thinking! I figured if I was meant to go through life miserable, then everyone else should be miserable too. You *Frivolities* women and your fulfilled lives rubbed me the wrong way. I treated you so poorly. I'm sorry for the wrong I've done your family, especially Moselle. When I saw her so in love with Eric, I was reminded of my own loss."

"Come on now, Kate. The Lord used it to His glory. Look how happy Moselle and Eric are now."

"Their love is one of the reasons for my bitterness over the years. A blind person could see how much Eric and Moselle loved each other when they were young. It hurt me so! Why couldn't Ted and I share that kind of love?"

Lanae blew a breath of pent-up air. "Know what you mean. I missed Keith something fierce after he died."

Kate went on as though Lanae hadn't spoken. "I'd

hear honeymoon stories and remember Teddy talking about taking me to white sandy beaches. Haven't given that a thought in years. I've never seen a white sandy beach."

Lanae had the sense Kate held herself together by a thread. She didn't interrupt Kate's pause.

"Well, I have to make it up somehow," she stood abruptly. "Maybe I'll become your best customer. I need to go back and choose a crocheted table runner for my great-niece."

"You know, I'm thinking of teaching Mia how to crochet. Would you like to learn?"

"Now, what in the world would I make?"

"Same things I do. I've made scarves for people and furniture, ecru bookmarks with white flowers for accent, cuddly critters for kids—from farm animals to teddy bears, rosettes, trims, granny square quilts, Christmas angels, stockings, trees, mittens, and slippers. In fact, I plan to make slippers for Mia since she hates to feels a seam in socks."

"Sounds like a load of yarn. I suppose I could crochet. Isn't there some program where quilts are made for sick children in the hospital?"

Lanae had to think of the day-to-day activities to keep her mind off Sage. "There is, and it's an excellent idea. I crochet blankets for that project. Kate, if crocheting isn't your cup of tea, maybe you can be influenced to make quilted blankets. The arthritis in Geneva's hands is getting worse. I think she has varied designs in loose blocks waiting to be constructed— double T, tumbling blocks, Sunbonnet Sue, dahlia designs. Just waiting to be sewn into quilts."

"I can already quilt, at least by machine. When shall we start?"

"How about tonight? And when you come, would you remind us we need to agree on Moselle's menu for men who shop in the store?"

****

Her mind raced as Lanae prepared for the Monday meeting. Her plan was to forgo the business aspect, which they could do later during inventory at the beginning of the year.

She set a wickless pine-scented candle on the warmer and grabbed her cordless phone out of its base with her other hand. She called Moselle and Geneva to give them a heads-up that Kate was joining them for crafts.

Moselle often gave in to her elders, but it was clear by her tone of voice, she wasn't wild about the idea of Kate's attendance.

"God is in the business of giving second chances," Lanae reminded her niece.

Lanae pictured Moselle raising her brow and pursing her lips. Resignation came through in her answer. "See you soon, then."

What do I have in life if I don't have faith? The belief God keeps His hand on me. He knew me before I was born. He'll know me through eternity. He has a purpose for my life and every life He creates.

But now Lanae doubted what exactly Sage had to do with her life. Maybe God had used her to bring the Tippin family secret to light and to mend the past. Having them meet Kate. Now wouldn't that be something?

Lanae began to wonder if living above *Frivolities* was God's long-term plan for her life—her life as a chapter in God's story. He knew the desires of her heart. She longed for a home in the country.

But could she settle for just any old place? "My preference is a place that comes along with a cowboy named Sage."

A blast of cold air on her ankles hit her the same time as Geneva's voice, "Don't you lock this door? And are you talking to yourself again?"

"Must have been talking so loud I didn't hear you."

"Mia wanted to come up the outside stairs so the snow muffled our steps."

"Sorry I didn't have them cleared."

"Hi, Aunt Lanae. I liked the snow on the steps." Mia, wearing a mini granny-square scarf Lanae had crocheted, knocked her stocking cap off as she unwound the scarf from her neck.

"See how she wears it under the collar of her coat?" Geneva commented as she unzipped Mia's coat. "She can't stand the coat collar next to her skin."

Mia shrugged out of her coat and kicked off her boots.

"Tags scratch my neck, too, sweetie," Lanae said to Mia. Lanae gathered Mia and Geneva's coats. She nudged Geneva in passing. "I see she's not wearing socks yet."

"No way. Not even in the dead of winter. She claims they wrinkle, and she can feel the balled-up mess with every step."

"Well, I'll have to do something about making her seamless slippers."

The phone interrupted their banter. Lanae bundled coats in one arm to pick up the handset with the other. Moselle. "Aunt Lanae, Kate called me to pick her up, so we'll be a little late."

Lanae said another silent prayer that Kate would put things right with Moselle, for Kate's sake. Moselle was making the effort to put the past behind her and forgive Kate. Since she and Eric were now married, what did Kate's tongue matter? It may matter to Kate, who sought to be done with the past.

Look who's talking.

The incident took place near the end of Moselle and Eric's senior year of high school. They grew up together then fell in love. But Eric's teen hormones kicked into gear and when Moselle wouldn't give in to what he wanted, she got out and started to walk back to town in the wee hours. Eric picked her up, but Moselle wasn't inside the house before Kate Rawlins, who was walking her dog, saw Moselle with a torn blouse.

Lanae finished out loud, "But it was between those two."

"You're talking to yourself again. What were you mumbling about when I came in?" Geneva asked.

"Oh, trying to sort life out according to God's plan. I don't want to be like the old gal who lamented over all the things she would or wouldn't do as she aged and looked back. If I had my life to live over again, I want no regrets. I want to know I was relaxed, playful, and even silly. I want to go out being known for having a life full of joy, for not getting hung up on the small stuff that didn't matter a whit. I want to go out assured I hadn't embarrassed my Jesus."

"Relax, sis. Look what happened to me when I quit trying to work so hard to do the right thing."

"Rainn." Lanae joined Geneva on his name. They were laughing when Moselle and Kate came in.

Kate held the door open for Moselle, who toted in the used sewing machine Lanae had found at a garage sale. "Mom's been showing me sewing tricks, Aunt Lanae. Thanks again for the machine. It's an awesome wedding gift."

Lanae nodded, tested the looks on their faces, and concluded Kate and Moselle had mended their fences.

She turned her attention to Moselle, who prattled away as she unloaded her fabric and trims. Geneva looked on with a proud mother's grin.

Moselle spoke with enthusiasm. "You know I got to looking at the *Frivolities* aprons. Mom, Aunt Lanae, your choice of the nine-patch quilt design, the pockets and the embroidered logo is super for us. I decided to order some plain aprons to embellish for sale. Maybe they'll be the shop's Valentine's offering. We can add the *Frivolities* logo on the edge, maybe, only make it smaller than the designs on our aprons."

"I can do that in a single embroidery stitch," Lanae added.

Moselle held up her newest apron experiment in mint green with a hot pink scalloped hem. "I figured, Aunt Lanae, you could embroider pink posies and white daisies on the waistband—"

"You can do that on the machine, I'll bet," Lanae said, "or, I could edge the apron with crochet trim."

Geneva picked up an apron in bright yellow. "This would be perfect background for a purple appliquéd animal."

"What can I do?" Mia asked

"I'm so glad you want to help, Mia. How about you join Kate and me for a crochet lesson?"

Mia's eyes rounded. "Right now, Aunt Lanae?"

"No better time than the present. Kate, please join

Mia and me. Let's check out my crochet supplies. Hope you're up to this. We *Frivolities* women can get carried away when we're doing our craft thing."

Lanae knelt to be eye level with Mia, and sang, "I love you a bushel and a peck."

Mia giggled and finished the vocal rhyme with action. "And a hug around the neck," she said, nearly choking Lanae.

Lanae straightened and took a deep breath. She hadn't thought of Sage since preparing for the evening with the women. No time to ponder over him now. She had work to do.

"First thing, let's check out what we need to get started. You can even call them crochet tools." Lanae led them to her stash of supplies. "We're going to begin with simple stitches that will make a scarf. First, there is yarn in different worsted-weights. I go with medium. What colors do you want?"

Kate chose a lavender-blue that reminded Lanae of Sage's eyes. And Ted's. Mia selected bright purple.

"Next is the crochet hook. We'll use size G. These come in fun colors, too, and I like them because they're not heavy. Later, we'll need needles with big eyes. They're all plastic, Mia. And we'll need scissors."

Before long, their crazy game of naming people and their occupations accompanied the lessons and the handwork.

"A seamstress called Ima Dressmaker?" Moselle accelerated her sewing machine pedal.

"I had a Dr. Gastro McCarver once in Omaha," Kate said as she fumbled with her crochet hook.

"Well, crack me up," Lanae put in. "How about Miss Dewey the librarian. Or a salesman named M.E. Sel."

"Dr. Toothaker is a dentist. For real. My mommy said." It was one of the few times anyone heard Mia mention her mother, who was a victim of homicide, a case that remained open to this day.

They all stared at the child.

Mia's input, her presence in the moment, thrilled Lanae. She caught Geneva's eye as she responded, "That's so right, big girl. OK, now, are you and Kate ready to begin? First, hold the crochet hook in your right hand and make a slip knot on the crochet hook. Like this."

They followed directions. Lanae was continually preoccupied, wondering what Sage was doing.

"I thought my thumbs were as big as a hand when I stared at this machine needle the first time," Moselle said. "By the way, Aunt Lanae, before the wedding you were talking about the singles ads. Did you ever answer somebody like Dr. Looooooove, matchmaker?"

All needles fumbled due to their laughter.

Moselle got out of her chair to tune in country music and put water on to heat for cocoa and tea.

Lanae's train of thought froze when she heard lyrics about loving someone who didn't feel the same way. It took everything she had to gain focus enough to shake off the helpless feeling of not knowing the outcome of her relationship with Sage. She would not give up her fight for a place in Sage's life.

She focused on her task. "Let's make your chain stitch, Mia."

"Practice, practice, practice," Geneva inserted in a sing-song voice.

"I'm tired of practicing. Mia has had enough crocheting. I'm going to read my book now. I get stickers and my name on the wall in my room at school."

"You go right ahead, dear. You may take your book, and go in the bedroom where it's quiet," Lanae told Mia.

"First, Mia wants a ponytail in my hair like my ponies," she announced to Moselle.

"How can that work?" Lanae, closest to the girl, ran her fingers through Mia's hair. "Your hair is about as short as a bobcat's tail instead of a pony's mane."

With a puzzled look, Mia pulled away from Lanae and turned to Geneva.

Geneva hugged Mia and raised a brow at Lanae over the riotous mop. "Aunt Lanae told a joke, Mia. She wasn't laughing at you, and she didn't mean to hurt your feelings. You have beautiful curls made just the way God wants them to be. Right now they won't work in ponytails until your hair grows longer." Mia allowed Geneva to escort her into the bedroom for quiet reading. Geneva returned to the room.

"Now we can talk about men," Moselle said, giving both earrings a good bounce before preparing the tea.

"Ah, the honeymoon lingers," Kate said. "But, oh, I was supposed to ask if you've any ideas about men shopping in *Frivolities*?"

"Would you believe honeymoon is one of the words I've used on the 'Men's Menu for Making Points?' I've made a copy for each of us, even you, Kate." Moselle grabbed cardstock prints from her tote.

"'Men's Menu for Making Points.' Catchy." *I need to run that by Sage.*

As she handed the designed sheets to each woman, Moselle bubbled with enthusiasm. "It's such a glorious thing for our lives to be controlled by the

Spirit. God created quite a thing when he designed men and women for a marriage relationship. It's great, but I may be more spiritually connected to Eric when he's praying than when I'm held in his arms."

"I already have that connection with Rainn," Geneva said. "When I was in my forties I thought women were somehow supposed to wrinkle up and fade away."

"I should surely hope not." Lanae's laughter rang out with her sister's.

"Don't believe it for a second. God wants us to be full of joy, to enjoy life as He offers it," Geneva continued.

"All you have to do is waste your adult life to realize that the life you have is a gift from God. I hope I can make up for it somehow," Kate finished with a sniff.

"But, Kate, remember the Lord meets us right where we are. Once we confess, we begin anew," Moselle said.

"When I got sick, I believed the best had already happened," Lanae said. "I took the motto to live like I was dying, so I tried to cherish each moment. Anyone can overcome their plight in life, so I'm not too gung-ho at becoming empathetic with Sage over the way he clings to Becca's memory." She paused to follow Geneva's efficient movements in the kitchenette. Then she continued. "After I got well, I realized how lonely I was. I thought no one depended on me."

"But we do, Aunt Lanae!" Moselle handed Lanae a glass of spicy cider and joined her on the butter leather couch.

Lanae continued her oral introspection. "I was self-sufficient even before Keith was killed, but I looked around and saw that no one needed me. Geneva had Rainn. Moselle had Eric. Look at Kate here. She could crochet items for *Frivolities*. Or she can use her gifts by contributing to service projects."

Geneva disappeared to bring Mia back in and sat her down on a stool at the counter.

"As much as I love *Frivolities*, it doesn't compare to the call of the great outdoors. Once I saw where Sage lives and how he spends his days, well, I felt so alive. I may be discontent with some things in my life, and sounding maudlin right now, but in this moment, and I have to say it out loud, I am content to be alive."

She bounced up, trying not to spill her hot drink. "I propose a toast to family and new friendships that span five generations." Lanae raised her mug of spiced tea and clinked four varied hot drinks in turn.

"What's a generation, Moselle?" Mia expected the answer before she would take a drink of her cocoa.

The telephone rang, and as Lanae went to answer, she could hear Moselle speaking to her sweet soon-to-be stepsister..

Lezlie jumped right in without preamble when Lanae said hello. "Jax is way crazy about Dad moving to Florida come spring. Did the two of you talk about his plans at all?"

Lanae's insides tumbled like a tower of children's blocks, and her leaden stomach stayed on the floor.

Could she do anything to make Sage stay in Nebraska?

Was he meant to stay?

17

Sage counted three rings. He heard the joy for life and pleasure of her business when she answered. *"Frivolities.* This is Lanae. May I help you?"

"Hey, there. Thanks for stating your name. You and Geneva sound just alike."

She laughed softly and he pictured her animation and wondered what crazy color she was wearing.

"Thanks again for coming back to the house and letting me unload my family's grisly past."

He pictured Lanae in Frivolities, surrounded by flashy merchandise, and blending right in with her own colorful flair. He was captivated by the way she used her unique tastes and gifts for her family and their business.

"I guess you know I'm taking Lezlie and Jax on vacation?"

"I understand it's something you do." Her voice lost its exuberance.

"Right. I'm not so excited about my objective for this particular place any more, though." He wanted to say so many things. Like, *because of you, I put Becca's pictures all away. I love you now, Lanae. I believe we have Becca's blessing.*

After a pause, he went on. "This is a huge favor to ask, and I'm really sorry, but it's kind of an emergency."

"You know the answer is yes, if I can. What's wrong, Sage?"

"The neighbor who usually feeds the horses when I'm gone fell on that ice we had. He can't come over while tussling with a pair of crutches, attempting to do chores. I just checked with Lorinda, but she's sick with a virus. Do you think—"

"I'd love to. Just walk me through it."

"Oh, what a relief. You won't have to come over until Christmas night. I usually feed and water twice a day, but I can't expect you to do that with your business and everything."

"Sage, it's no problem at all. I'd love to come down and do it. I imagine we'll have a slump between holidays. Beth can come in to the shop if we need extra help. Or even Kate, if you can imagine that one."

"Sounds like you've got yourself a new friend. Well, we're taking off from Omaha early evening. Let me tell you where everything is."

All the while they talked his mind was on plans to cancel the realtor appointments in Florida. He was sick at heart over the earlier decision to look for property while there. That was before Lanae had come into his life. Sage wondered at the ache in his chest. He already missed Lanae. Before he was ready, it was time to end the call.

"I guess this is good-bye for now," he said.

"Better than a note anytime."

"Oh, I don't know. Maybe I'll write to you and rub in how much fun I'm having on the white sandy beach, as my uncle used to say." He wanted to hold her in his arms, reluctant to break their connection.

But he'd save that confession for later. Somehow, Sage managed to disconnect.

And her words came back. *Just imagine, Sage, if you had to leave your land and move.*

He'd answered that he'd be lost and angry.

****

Later in the day, he greeted Lezlie and Jaxson. They were both reserved, Jax with a chip on his shoulder.

He'd heard the grumbling before, but he totally lost it when Jaxson said, "I s'pose Mom'll put me through another five days as structured as a day in preschool."

"Give her a break, son. She works hard to even earn a vacation for the two of you."

"Why couldn't we have a normal Christmas like normal people?"

Because I can't face normal holidays. He made no verbal answer.

Traffic on I-80 to Omaha was heavy. Most likely, with people working late to wrap things up at the office or doing the traveling themselves. He absent-mindedly watched the signs for Eppley Airfield, noted the Qwest Center and Abbott Drive, thought how much easier to go this way than the interstate. That route drove him nuts having to drive south past the airport in order to arrive at the terminal from the north. He shot a cursory look toward Carter Lake and eventually parked in long-term.

Conversation on the shuttle was excited. The Diamonds were the only riders leaving for the holiday without plans to see family.

Deep down Sage figured he was leaving family behind.

Could Lanae possibly miss him as much as he missed her already?

****

Soak it up, this adventure called life.

The sound of gentle rain woke Lanae in the dark, pre-dawn hours of Christmas Eve morning. She was transported and disoriented, believing she and Keith were together. Her senses were alive to her surroundings. She listened for his deep breathing, inhaled the fresh, cold air blowing through the open window. Snuggled into the comforting warmth of another body, it was good to feel so alive.

Lanae stretched one arm around her pillow, pulling it close, and extended the other.

The sheet was cold, the spot next to her empty.

But it was too late. Keith hadn't stayed. He'd climbed on the skid steer loader and met the Lord.

"Don't go." The sound of her voice crashed her into wakefulness.

Then she remembered. Keith was gone. She was in the loft above *Frivolities*. A unique place not created for her, but for Moselle.

She took advantage of that place between wakefulness and sleep; dimly recalled the previous night and how the air had felt almost balmy. She had left a window cracked at the back of the loft. The air was now crisp, but she held on to the security of married love. She snuggled deeper into the memory foam mattress that squished and cradled her now.

And wondered if she'd ever share a bed with a

loving husband again.

Could she remain content staying in town, living in the loft, while her heart yearned to be at the acreage with Sage?

But Sage was gone as well. His absence may only be a vacation for now, but if Lezlie was right, Sage could soon be gone forever.

He planned to move, so who knew how much time they had left together?

Dare I say, "Don't go" to Sage?

Lanae opened her eyes and made out the shadowed shapes of furniture. She tossed back the warm mauve quilt and the teal sheet in one swoop then padded across the cold wood floor to shut the window.

Back under the covers, she tried to find warmth and comfort.

Her mind circled back to Sage. Was he the present in her life?

But Sage would have to learn to live in the present.

Her thoughts flitted around like a butterfly searching for the best flower to sip on. Lanae's mind swooped from one dear person, or subject, to another until it landed on secrets.

Secrets.

She'd kept her one-night stand all to herself for years.

Sage had kept Uncle Ted's identity to himself long enough.

Kate, aka Katherine, had kept her love for Ted secreted in her heart for even longer than Lanae could imagine.

I can do this. I want to look back someday knowing this tumultuous tumbling in the head was all worth it.

What was the weather like in Florida where Sage and his family were vacationing? She pictured herself holding hands with Sage, walking on an endless white sandy shore surrounded by nothing but blue sky and sea. The imagined tropical breeze engulfed her.

She shook it off and reached for her Bible.

****

Consider it pure joy, my brothers, whenever you face trials of many kinds.—James 1:2

Christmas Eve service at Faith Bible Church left Lanae with a hollow feeling rather than the promise of God's gift.

On the church steps, Geneva said, "You seem far away. Are you feeling all right?"

"Oh, sure. I got all wrapped up in the words of the carols, but as soon as we stepped outside, I wondered if I'll ever get a chance for a life with Sage. Is our time over?" She made sure Rainn was talking to someone else before she leaned in and said, "I regret not getting the chance to kiss him silly before he left. He couldn't possibly forget me if I'd branded him."

The next morning, Christmas Day, during a quiet spell in the kitchen, she said to Geneva, "My mind and heart have been far, far away today."

"Let me guess, still on an imaginary warm sandy beach with a cowboy?"

Lanae left the family gathering mid-afternoon, giving herself time to do the chores on the acreage, planning to return before full dark set in.

She dallied when she got to the barn. The setup was efficient, down to the stall mucking, thanks to the vet who had once lived there. Complete with bins, cubbyhole-type cupboards and tins to keep out rodents, the layout of supplies made quick work of feeding the four horses.

When Lanae smelled molasses sweetening the oats, it took her right back to her former life. Did Sage mix it in to treat his horses while he was gone?

Lanae's elbow caught the edge of a tattered spiral notebook and knocked it to the concrete floor. The skewed top and bottom wires reminded her of the Torn Notebook sculpture on University Campus in Lincoln. This deep blue cover was stained with who knew what. Curiosity had always gotten the best of her. She couldn't resist. She opened the cover...just a peek. She'd only glance at a few pages.

Most of the notes related to horses. Lanae ran a finger over the cursive writing, sometimes in blue ink, sometimes in black. The words she read, written in what she assumed to be Sage's script, could be applied to people as well.

It's all in the body language.

Horses are a flight animal. Humans are fight animals.

Horses have personalities: friend, loyal, trustworthy, hard-working, dedicated; fearful, lazy, skittish, moody, cantankerous, ornery.

Use your faculties when you work: awareness, compassion, forgiveness, confidence.

Lanae pictured Sage in the saddle and the lay of the acreage. Many horse trainers use a round pen with portable gates. Sage preferred the open space and followed God's corral—creek or contours of the land.

The same patience he used while he rode showed in the precise handwriting.

"Talk" to the horse with your legs.

"Feel" the horse's energy—back off with the pressure of calf, hand, or leg if there's resistance.

Reward the horse when he "listens."

Sage's voice echoed through the written words.

I need to listen when the horse "speaks."

The horse moves into pressure, not away from it, and a horse learns with its body. OBSERVE.

Use the hackamore—Lanae pictured a rawhide noseband without a bit—on Freckles.

She thumbed through the pages, wondering if Sage referred to them when he worked with the horses' owners or with Jaxson.

She gasped when she saw her name, any intention of controlling her curiosity flew right out the window.

This entry wasn't written evenly on a fine blue line, but scrawled on the page diagonally.

Lanae's lips taste like sweet grass to a thirsty soul.

And lower on the same page he had written, with what looked like a trembling hand, *I don't remember what Becca tastes like. And I didn't know I missed being close to a lovely woman.*

The words kicked Lanae in the heart.

Back to reading, she snorted.

That woman poked her nose where it didn't belong, being so tenacious about the letters. I thought I was done looking back. But isn't that what I did? Peeked at the past, every time I studied Becca's picture?

Lanae turned the notebook to the open page that had first caught her eye, setting it in place so as to look undisturbed, and left the barn.

He wasn't immune to her after all.

She shivered. Winter's chill seeped through her coat.

Sage had asked that she also go through the house

each evening to turn off burning lights and turn on different lights. The key was inside the garage, right where he said it would be. She left her boots at the door and stepped inside. She attended to the lights, turning on the light that shone in the main living area and then she yelped.

Becca's picture wasn't on the mantle.

She flew down the stairs and through the basement rooms, taking care to hit alternate lights as she hurried.

She braved the master bedroom next. Inside the door, she held her breath, turned on the light. Eyes fixed on the stand next to the bed, she expected to see Becca's image, set off by a fancy frame. She didn't see any photos of Becca.

There was nothing on the night stand but a lamp, a clock, and a Bible.

A Bible?

Lanae couldn't resist a peek inside the front of the worn burgundy leather cover, and read: *"We read to know we're not alone." [C.S. Lewis in* Shadowlands]

She sank onto the edge of the bed.

Thank you, Lezlie. I assume this was Becca's Bible.

Well, Lord, no matter what lies ahead for he and I, Sage knows he's not alone as long as he has Your Word.

****

Christmas night

My Dearest Sage,

I miss you. I don't know if you miss me, yet, but my soul is reaching out to yours. I know without a doubt you should be here by my side.

You drew me to yourself the moment I looked into your eyes.

Then while reading Kate's letters to your Uncle Ted, I was so emotionally affected. At the time, I felt her yearnings, and I longed to be with a man again. Passion stirred anew.

At this time in my life I've never been more certain of anything, even Frivolities, *up to this point. God wants me to love you.*

He blessed us both with young love, through your Becca and my Keith.

He carried us through our losses.

He's blessing us now with each other.

I love you, Sage.

I want to spend the rest of my days with you.

How could you possibly love me? I've wondered. I'm often too outspoken for my own good. I'm opinionated and scatterbrained. I'm snoopy because I'm interested in other people.

I used to wonder why God saved me from terminal illness. Now I believe it was ordained for me to spend the rest of my life with you. But you won't be free to love me the way I need, until you make things right with our Lord.

Have you let Becca go? God holds her safe, and that should be a comfort.

And if we aren't meant to be, I wish you enough of whatever God offers you in life–especially, enough peace to continue on to the end—so you can find contentment, as I finally have.

*Now I'll sign off the same way Katherine did, with as many*XXXXXXXXXXXXXXXXXXXXXXXXXXXXXXXXXX XXXXXXXXXXXXXXXXXXXXXXX*'s as I can make my fingers X.*

Loving you forever,
Lanae

P.S. I noticed Becca's pictures are gone. My curiosity will wait until your return.

Lanae mentally toured the ranch house, planning on where she'd place the letter. She decided to set it on top of Sage's mail stack so he'd see it first thing when he walked into the kitchen after his trip.

18

Sage stomped sand off his boots onto the rattan mat at the beach side of the condo. He was such a cowboy. Any other guy vacationing in Florida would be wearing flip-flops. Or going barefoot.

Vacations were supposed to be relaxing, but his mind was back in Nebraska. With Lanae. He kept picturing her, full-of-life, doing normal Christmas things with her family.

He wanted to call her, just to hear her voice.

Then he heard Lezlie speaking and figured she was talking to Jaxson. But through the glass at the front of the condo, he spied Jax talking to a pretty blonde girl.

Lezlie must be on the phone. Talking to Lanae?

"My dad's name is Sage," Lezlie said. "We live in Nebraska, and I think you might be my uncle."

He swung toward his daughter. "What in the world?"

Lezlie turned, phone in hand, smile an ocean wide. "I looked in the telephone book. Lanae suggested it. Anyway, you wanna talk to Ted Tippin?"

She offered the cell phone to Sage. He stood as though rooted in cement.

Was he dreaming?

He automatically reached for the cell and put it to his ear.

"Hello? Hello?" came a voice from Sage's childhood.

His uncle Ted had to be at least seventy, but Sage recognized his voice.

Nothing is coincidental with God. Sage's mother's voice echoed in the back of his mind.

He gathered enough strength to answer, "Uh, yeah."

"Sage?" He heard the shaky reply. "Sage Diamond, my sis Violet's boy?"

"Yeah. It's me. I guess we should get together."

It turned out that Ted Tippin lived on the other side of the highway, less than a mile away.

The whole thing was mighty hard for Sage to take in.

"I'd walk, but I might get killed like a guy from Nebraska did one time down here on vacation. I got all kinds of questions for you, son. When did your mother die? What have you been doing with your life? You'd better be a believer, boy, or I'll take a switch to ya."

They shared an uncomfortable laugh over the sick cliché, both knowing it was Earl Tippin who did the beating in the family. They agreed on a time to meet and ended the call.

In a daze, Sage tidied up the condo for his uncle's visit. He stacked a pack of cards and returned them to the box. He pictured Lanae handling the game in his home when the box spilled during the icy snowstorm.

Every couple should find a game they enjoy to while away quiet time in their old age. His mother's words revived from the past again. He hadn't recalled anything she said to him in longer than—he didn't know when. And that was twice in one day.

Had his mom known something he didn't?

Lezlie came up from behind and gave Sage a big squeeze. "You're nervous, aren't you, Dad?"

"Who wouldn't be? It's been a couple lifetimes since I've seen him. I've married and lost a wife. I have you and Jax. I'm hoping I'll see the same man who used to mean the world to me."

"Speaking of meaning the world, I haven't told you for a while, Dad. Thanks for all you've done for me. I know I was a brat more than I was a princess. And thanks for being such a terrific grandfather to Jaxson."

"I love him."

"I know, and your love means the world to me. Sorry you didn't have the kind of grandfather Jaxson's been blessed to have."

Searching for an answer that wouldn't cloud the exciting day, Sage caught the sun glinting on a windshield. He watched his uncle pull up to the drive. "My grandfather was an angry, mean man. No reason to talk about it. Just the way it was."

He and Lezlie walked out to stand by Jaxson. They all waited in the heat. The foreign smell of fish and sea vegetation permeated the air where they were shaded by the overhanging roof. Some unidentifiable bird sang, but the beauty of the song was chased away by the squawk of a gull.

No more time to reflect on their surroundings. Ted Tippin angled out of his nondescript car.

Sage recognized his uncle with no problem. When their gazes met, the matching lavender-blue eyes glistened with unshed tears. Ted carried muscular shoulders and a spry walk. His face was lined, yet glowed with healthy color.

"I would have known you anywhere. Uncle Ted,

meet my daughter, Lezlie. And grandson, Jaxson."

Ted opened his arms to Lezlie and said, "Thanks for calling, young lady. I'll be eternally grateful."

Ted turned and shook Jaxson's hand before Sage got his turn.

His hand was grasped in an iron band then Uncle Ted wrapped him in a bear hug. Lifted off his feet, Sage let the tears run unchecked. It took all he had not to let loose with a sob. After a time, muscular arms relaxed and the men stepped back, gazes reconnecting.

By unspoken agreement, the men walked right through the condo and on out to the seashore. They walked and talked until Lezlie called them in for dinner at the same time the orange ball of sun slipped below the horizon.

An hour later, Sage was replete, from more than nourishment.

Ted said, "Now that was a treat. Not often I get a home cooked meal these days. Mind if we have a little music now?"

Sage felt his eyes pool with moisture yet again. "How could I forget how you used to sing?"

"Jaxson, could you please bring my guitar from the car?" Ted asked.

"Sure. But, Grandpa?" Jaxson turned to Sage. "I've been thinking while you two have been getting to know one another again, it's like you're really here. You've been kind of far away, like a part of you was missing before. If you catch what I mean." Jaxson stopped, turning as red as the salsa he'd just devoured with a bag of chips.

"You're right, son. Reality means the past is done and we have to go on living. I have been distant. Thanks for your honesty. We're never too old to change." Sage ruffled Jaxson's hair. "Now, how about fetching that guitar?"

In no time at all, Uncle Ted led them outside to the veranda. He started with "The All Day Song," which he said he'd learned in Alaska. He sang it by himself and then taught the others.

He went on to "This is My Father's World" and Sage said, "How could I have forgotten one of my favorite hymns?"

"Your grandma liked that one, too. God's in control no matter how messed up we sinners manage to get things. All I have to do is come outside and here He is. The birds, the sun, the moon, the sea...all His, since He made them." Ted went on to play and sing other nature songs.

Sage longed for the nature of home, where his peace meant prairie flowers and the whisper of wind through the cottonwoods. Life in Nebraska had its own sounds, smells, rhythms. How had he even considered leaving?

He missed Lanae, but had he not come on this trip, he would have never found his Uncle Ted. God sure made life a mystery at times.

Jaxson grew bored with the old songs and turned in. Then Lezlie bid them goodnight after a couple more camp songs.

Eventually, Ted stood and rested his guitar against the outside wall. "Let's walk, unless you're tired like the others."

"Naw. My mind is wide awake."

As they meandered, moonlight reflected off the water.

Ted eventually asked, "How did your ma die?"

Sage repeated the story he had told Lanae when

they took their trail ride.

"Then she went out doing what she enjoyed," Ted said.

"A wise lady friend said the same thing. Mom died the way she had lived. On the farm, out in the open, caring for critters."

Ted slanted a deep look at Sage. "Now, tell me about your wife."

"I didn't pay any attention when Becca complained about how fat her belly felt to her, or the squeezing cramps that took her to her knees at times. I just figured it was a female thing, way out of my element. The malignant tumors started in the ovaries."

"Suppose they did surgery?"

Sage picked up where he'd left off. "Right. But the cancer was discovered too late. They took her ovaries. Then the cancer was found in the fallopian tubes and elsewhere."

They jumped back from a foamy wave and staggered like a couple drunks in a lopsided circle.

When they stopped dodging the tide, Sage continued. "Once they discovered the malignant cells had spread, I couldn't believe how fast it went. Becca's cancer was in the tissue. She went through radiation and started chemo. That whole time passed in a blur. It made me so mad that I couldn't do a thing to change it."

He kicked driftwood out of his path. "I haven't gotten over my mad. She didn't want to be sick anymore, hated the treatment. So she decided no more chemo. She went pretty fast after that."

"Imagine it was tough for you to watch. As Christians, we don't go through something that horrible by ourselves. When it's sudden we can't prepare ourselves, but it's a whole other story to watch someone die."

Sage believed in the salvation Jesus offered, but he'd been broadsided by his wife's death. And that had delayed his recovery.

His choice, not God's.

God had not left Sage.

He led their steps back the way they had come, paying no attention to their surrounding smells or sounds. "It was such a nightmare that when she got really bad, I think I blocked out reality. The days and nights just blurred together while I took care of her as long as I could on my own."

"The way I see it, love is threefold. No doubt it's physical, but that craziness settles down. It's spiritual, a calling of one soul to another. And it's mental because the bottom line is choice. Love is a choice rather than a feeling."

As Ted spoke, Sage believed he could finally put Becca totally in the past, tuck her away in a corner of his heart, along with all the pictures he'd hidden away in the trunk.

Lanae was his future. "Uncle Ted, have you ever loved someone?"

"I have. And I lost her. She didn't pass from illness, though. I made a choice that separated us. I made a choice that ruined any chance with her."

As though Ted could read minds, he said, "Now tell me about this woman you're so connected with now."

"That's a loaded order. I came down here expecting to find a home to move to, and all I've done is watch time pass, waiting to get back home to her. Listening to you, I feel that tri-fold connection with one woman. Her name is Lanae Petersen, and she is something else. So full of life, it hurts to be around her sometimes. Lanae and her sister Geneva, and Geneva's daughter Moselle, own a woman's shop in Platteville. She's a country gal, used to live on a ranch. I advertised the dressing table that once was Grandmother Juanita's, and Lanae saw the dresser ad. When she started the refinishing, she found letters in a secret place." Sage drew a breath, wishing he could see his uncle's face clearly in the dark. He switched gears. "Do you listen to country music?"

At Ted's questioning nod, Sage asked, "What do you think of the song, 'Live Like You Were Dying?'"

"It's loaded, but right-on. If a guy's facing death, I mean."

"Right. Lanae claims it as a motto. She had a disease that could have been terminal. Says the first time she heard the lyrics, her heart felt like a hand squeezed her chest cavity." Sage felt his heart clench, as though Lanae was holding it in her fist. "Anyway, she used that verve to search out who wrote such impassioned letters, secreted away in an old dresser. All the while Lanae strove for answers surrounding the letters, she was especially curious about finding out who Katherine and her beloved Teddy were. I grew to like her more. And I fought harder to keep the family secret."

And here the secret was. In the flesh. In the process of discovery, I somehow lost my connection to the memory of my Becca.

Sage could only guess at what was going on in the older man's mind. "Well, now's as good a time as any to tell you another story. I hope this one's got a happy ending."

Uncle Ted remained silent.

Sage went on to tell how the *Frivolities* women used the family dressing table to display one of the letters. "Katherine Rawlins, now known as Kate, read the letter in the store and went all to pieces about losing her Teddy."

Ted gasped and stumbled. Probably been holding his breath since the first time Sage said the name Katherine.

Sage caught his uncle by the arm. "Yes. Your Katherine. Lezlie's probably already called home about finding you. If I know those women, they're planning a romantic reunion between you and Katherine Rawlins."

Uncle Ted shook his head repeatedly. He appeared too overcome to speak. Close to the rear of the condo now, Sage saw moisture pooling in his uncle's eyes.

Finally, Sage said, "And I have the letter you wrote Grandma from Alaska."

He couldn't say what he had expected, but a monotone question from his uncle with no apparent emotion, wasn't it.

"Didja tell anybody?"

"Only Lanae. Right before we came down here."

"Well now, I'd say it's about time I started living in the days I have left, and make a one-way trip to Nebraska. Way past time I face the music. Take lawful responsibility for my impassioned crime."

Sage felt like he'd taken a left to the jaw. His uncle wasn't the only one to live in the past. Sage had been sidetracked, locked in his head with Becca.

If a seventy-year-old man with murder in his background could take a chance on the future, so could he.

"If you can change the pattern of your life, dear uncle, I can, too. Something's been wrong in the realm of my thinking. For too long I've listened to a mocking negative voice instead of the still small voice of the Holy Spirit nudging me to get on with my life."

****

For I have learned to be content whatever the circumstances. — Philippians 4:11

Lanae lingered at the acreage. Sage would soon be home. She'd miss feeding the horses and walking through the rooms of his home. Coming to the acreage had been such a blessing. She'd left both letters she'd written to Sage with his mail. She couldn't say exactly when it hit, but she had come to realize she could be content wherever God chose for her to be at any given moment.

With or without Sage and his home in the country, she'd given it her best shot.

Lanae felt giddy. Her heart soared within her and took flight on the imaginary score of a Hollywood musical. She knew the giddy emotion would pass. Love was played out over the years in actions that spoke so much louder than words or hormones.

As deep as her love for Sage, she knew where she stood at this particular stage of her life.

"I don't have to miss the country. I can find a country connection within a few miles of Platteville. Surely there's a horse or two I can visit near me there," she announced to Snorty at feeding time.

She'd talked to the Lord often. She prayed for Sage

and his family's safe return. And above all, Lanae prayed that Sage would learn to be content and count his blessings, whether he stayed on the acreage or actually moved to a place similar to where he'd been vacationing in Florida.

****

On their last morning in Florida, Sage walked the shore, singing the same songs his uncle had reintroduced to him. He studied the horizon, wishing the expanse of the sea could lift the weight of unvoiced emotion. Who would have thought a man's head could hold such heavy, unspoken thoughts?

He owed Lezlie.

He owed Jaxson.

He owed Lanae.

Sage sang praises to the Lord from the depths of his soul.

He couldn't owe God for his inattention over the years, but he could let God meet him today, finally accept the gift of God's sovereignty. Sage could no longer question. God is God. Period. He gives and He takes away. Amen.

But he did owe his Uncle Ted, to help make things right in both their lives.

Sage wanted to introduce Lanae to his uncle's guitar and hear her join them in praise singing.

He hadn't told Lanae he'd canceled the realtor appointments. He wanted to see her face, her open joy, when he told her he wasn't about to move.

Nebraska was his home.

His family would return to Nebraska.

He vowed to use every resource he could to

uncover what the law needed, to set the record straight as far as his grandfather's death was concerned.

Eric and Rainn, tight in the community as respected firefighters, might be tight with the sheriff's department as well.

Could he be charged with being an accessory after the fact for withholding the letter as evidence? He'd deal with whatever he had to face, going through it with God.

"Surely, You meet us where we are, Lord. Seems to me You've waited a long time for me to return to You. But time is as meaningless to you as a footprint of sand underneath my feet here on the beach. Well, I'm ready for a new beginning."

Sage scanned the horizon once again. He couldn't find descriptive names for all the colors of blue he saw. "Psalm 95 says the sea is Yours, You made it. What a mighty God you are."

Sea sounds, sand, ocean smells, and shore air equaled a tranquil surrounding. It was a place for a soul to find peace. He packed it all away. The memory would bring him right back here where he laid his soul out before the Lord.

Sage bent to pick up a broken seashell. He drew a heart in the sand. Then he wrote "I love Lanae." He lost his balance, laughed to find himself on his seat instead of his haunches.

It's true. Somehow his subconscious heart had known the extent of his emotions before his conscious mind had.

"You are indeed an awesome God. Please forgive me for my anger. Thank You beyond measure for Lezlie and her search for Uncle Ted. Thank You for our reunion. Now, I ask that You give me the right words to pass on to Lanae. Thank You for bringing Lanae into our lives, and give me the ability to show her enough love to last the rest of our lives." He ended his time with His Lord on the beach in song, this time, the Lord's Prayer, remembering Lanae's rich alto voice.

He had to tell Lanae. Now. He trotted back to the beach condo. But instead of picking up the phone, he drew a pen from his pocket. And Sage poured out his heart.

December 28

My dear lovely, lively, Lanae,

We're still here on vacation on the beach. But there's only one place in the world I want to be, and that's next to you.

Thank you for putting up with my stubborn will. I wanted to continue through life as an observer, but I doubt that's God's plan for me. You helped me find myself again, to choose once more to let God direct my thoughts and my actions, to allow Him to be the steering wheel of my life.

Thank you for allowing yourself to feel Katherine's pain and her passion.

Thank you for your relentless curiosity and determination to discover Uncle Ted's identity, which helped me discover my own.

Thank you for showing me I needed to face my heritage and live today in order to face tomorrow instead of being lost in the past. By bringing the past into the present and then leaving it again, I have more to give my daughter and grandson.

And I should have more honesty to give you all.

Thank you for your affinity toward treasured practices

of the past. One of my vows to you is that as long as I am of sound mind, I promise to write you a love letter on the anniversary of our marriage. (If you'll have me.)

Since we met in late fall, I'm wondering if you bare your toes in warm weather. I'd like to polish your toes, enjoy a new experience, as a little something for the two of us to look forward to doing together.

I'll love you as long as I draw breath.

You and our Lord are the choices I make for going through the rest of my tomorrows.

When I return, I'm bringing a grand surprise.

Sage

P.S. Cause I love you a bushel and a peck. You bet your pretty neck, I do.

****

"For I know the plans I have for you," declares the Lord, "plans to prosper you and not to harm you, plans to give you hope and a future." — Jeremiah 29:11

Sage meditated on the Bible verse one last time before closing the Bible, courtesy of a worldwide ministry that placed the Good Book in rented rooms, and turned to zip his carry-on.

"Sorry, Dad." Lezlie giggled when Sage jumped and lost his grip.

"About what?"

"Well, I didn't mean to snoop, but I saw the packet of letters in your carry-on after we got here. You didn't zip it up and it was right there in the closet. Anyway, since the letters really belong to Uncle Ted, I put them in a scrapbook with plastic sleeves for him to look at during the flight. Or whenever he's ready. He'll probably want privacy."

"It's a beautiful gift," Sage said, nodding at the book in Lezlie's folded arms. "And so thoughtful. I'm proud of you."

Lezlie shrugged off the compliment. "Thought it'd be a nice Christmas gift for him, even if it is many years late."

"We're never too old to appreciate gifts given with love. With God, you know, a future and a hope are ageless. This is a priceless gift, Lezlie. Thank you for putting it together for him."

"What'd you do for me?" Jaxson entered the conversation as he slid into the room on an imaginary surfboard.

"Not you, carrot-top." Lezlie handed the scrapbook to Sage before attempting to get her son in a headlock. He dodged and turned to crash right into Uncle Ted.

"Hold up there. What's all the fuss?"

"Lezlie put this together for you," Sage said, presenting the gift to Ted.

Ted peeked inside. Moisture pooled in his eyes. He hugged Lezlie. "I don't know what to say, sweetheart. Glad my heart is strong. There are no words."

Sage felt his throat thicken with his own tears.

"Hey, Unc, thank Lanae Petersen." Lezlie patted Ted's shoulder and winked at Sage. "She came into Dad's life and shook up the whole family dynamics."

Sage spoke for the first time since Ted had walked into the room. "It was my personal goal after reading the letter you wrote to Grandma from Alaska that I'd protect my family from our violent secrets."

Ted smoothed a hand over the linen-like, handmade scrapbook cover. "I can relate to your empathy, son, and the reasons. Hypersensitivity can make us become callous. I've gone through years of avoiding people because of their problems, not wanting to get dragged down by their plights in life. I venture to guess that you got into spending time alone with your horses just so you didn't have to face other people's problems."

"You've guessed right. But, by isolating myself, I sank deeper into my shell. Never letting go of Becca, for instance."

But Lanae's shown me what I've been missing.

"What's this about Alaska?" Jaxson wanted to know.

"Let's all get something cold to drink and I'll tell you some stories," Ted said, with his gaze locked on Sage.

19

Now faith is being sure of what we hope for and certain of what we do not see. This is what the ancients were commended for. —Hebrews 11:1-2

Conversation rose and fell at the Todd's post-New Year's party. The noise level climbed in such measurable decibels that Sage searched the room to spy the culprit responsible. Moselle had turned up the volume by something she said, making others laugh louder. Geneva and Rainn stood in the circle, arms around the other.

Sage had brought his family. They'd made it as far as the diningroom table heaped with food. He had yet to spy Lanae.

When Eric first invited Sage to a party, it was for his Bible study fellowship. Sage had declined. He viewed his renewed fellowship with the Lord as a precious chapter in his life, and he stayed home a few days to spend a lot of time on his knees.

He surveyed the room. Uncle Ted roared with laughter over something Mia Harris must have said. Sage's heart hurt with pride over the way Jaxson had taken to the young girl. The teen had mumbled all the way to Platteville about being bored out of his skull. Just look at him now.

A collective "Ahhh" surrounded him, and he

wondered out loud, "What—"

On a sharp indrawn breath, Sage shut off his wandering thoughts when he saw the answer. Everyone else was moaning over the appearance of a gigantic cheesecake smothered in dark red cherries and chocolate curls surrounded by mounds of whipped cream.

His vision filled with the woman holding the platter.

Sage had never seen Lanae in a dress. She wore a dusky rose that draped into a flirty skirt he guessed she made herself. Her knees played peekaboo with a lacy crocheted hem as she took careful steps. She wore wild cowboy boots in turquoise and dusty pink. Stunning. He guessed where she bought them.

Once she set the treasure on the serving table, he stepped to her side.

Leaning in close, he said, "I'm sure this is a cliché, but you take my breath away."

"Ahhh. You're a poet."

Her eyes spoke volumes. But when the doorbell rang, they turned to watch an expected drama unfold.

Moselle greeted Kate but only had time to remove her coat before Ted threw his shoulders back and weaved his way across the room, oblivious of his audience.

Eric joined his wife Moselle near the door. Rainn pulled Geneva in closer to his side. Lezlie moved to stand near Jaxson and Mia.

Most adult eyes were glistening with moisture at the reunion taking place within their sight. God would help them recover, and overcome any obstacles to their remaining years on earth. Sage hoped to see many of them.

He swallowed a lump the size of a cow's cud at the sight of Ted opening his muscular arms for Katherine to walk into.

"All these years I thought I was the reason you had disappeared," Kate moaned with her voice muffled against Ted's chest. "I can't believe you're really here."

Ted said, "I am. what there is of me. If it meets your approval, I'd like to spend the rest of our lives talking about important things. Like how'd you stay so pretty all this time?"

Kate blushed and giggled like a girl. Her eyes sparkled with tears and the light of love. Her cheeks turned pink enough to match the soft color of her lipstick.

Sage grinned, wondering if his uncle had the urge to kiss off that lip color.

Jaxson rolled his eyes and turned to Mia. "This is too mushy for me. I hear you're learning to crochet. How about you tell me what you've been working on?"

"I would like that, Jaxson." Mia looked up at her crochet teacher as if she needed reassurance. At Lanae's nod, Mia told Jax all about the yarn stitches, the counting, the hook, and the scarf she was working on.

Jaxson made Sage proud, the way he listened to the little girl as if he was enthralled.

Moselle asked Kate and Ted if they'd like to go downstairs for privacy. Kate accepted spiced cider and Ted refilled his hot tea. They left the living room with their drinks and little space between them.

"Just because there's snow on the mountain doesn't mean the furnace went out," Rainn said.

The men enjoyed the impact of the statement more, and laughed longer, than the women.

Sage surveyed the room to make sure Jax hadn't overheard. He and Mia were now at the table eyeing Lanae's cheesecake.

They weren't the only ones with eyes glued to the table. Eric's huge yellow dog, Dear, had been allowed inside for the occasion. Her golden brown eyes matched her owner's, but were now drooping in a comical, begging pout. The St. Bernard/German shepherd drew Mia's delightful laughter.

Sage figured it was a wise move, having the Pluto-look-alike inside to occupy the younger guests.

Eric ambled to the buffet table, stuffed a mini crab cake into his mouth, and filled a plate with finger foods. "Behave yourself," he said as he scratched Dear behind the ears, "or you'll find yourself back outdoors."

Mia and Jaxson groaned their protests.

Lanae went back to the kitchen for a serving utensil, and he wondered if she was avoiding him. Except for the youngest in the group, the men and women were now segregated.

"So, Rainn, you need help with the drywall yet in your building?" Eric wanted to know.

"Eric's referring to the three-story, hundred-year-old building on Main Street I'm transforming into an art studio as well as gallery," Rainn explained for Sage. "I'll showcase the work of other Nebraska artists as well as my own stained glass art."

Sage said, "I hope it's as successful as the women's store."

"Thanks. I'm calling it *The Other One*. Eric, ole pal, it just so happens, the twelve-foot sheets of drywall were delivered this morning. So, first chance we're all free, you bet we can nail those babies up." Rainn turned back to Sage. "Speaking of the building, I've been thinking about the rear entrance and plan to do something similar to what I did behind *Frivolities*. I hear you've made yourself a landscaped rock garden, according to Lanae. Mind if I take a look some time?"

"Give me a call, and I'll show it to you. May and June are the best months for the flowers, but you come out and visit any time. I'll see if neighboring farmers have rocks to spare. Speaking of your art, the first time I pulled up to the gals' place off the alley, your stained-glass windmill caught my eye. You do fine work."

"Appreciate it. I try to put a cross in my pieces, big or small. To me, the cross reaches out like the arms of Jesus, welcoming the whole world with His unconditional love. Since the cross tip extends up, I like to look to the sky so I don't see the troubles of life around me."

"Hmm. You guys spread your belief. Eric uses his gifts by teaching Bible study and you through your art. I'm going to have to figure out how Jesus fits into the way I work with horses." His gaze landed on Mia and he wondered about children with special needs meeting his horses for therapy.

"You'll find it." Eric slapped him on the back.

"Speaking of finding," Rainn said with a lift of his brows, "there's someone in the kitchen I need to connect with."

As Sage sauntered through the door after Rainn, Lezlie said, "Looks like Dad is after the other sister in the kitchen."

Moselle joined Lezlie on the last three words. Their eyes met, and they said, "Jinx," simultaneously.

The women bumped hips as though they'd practiced the movement for years.

Until they laughed, Lanae and Geneva's voices couldn't be distinguished. Only those who knew them well could identify the speaker from another room. There were subtle nuances. Lanae now laughed as lightheartedly as Kate Rawlins had earlier, reminding Sage of her uninhibited happiness the day of their horseback ride.

Ripples of the sisters' laughter rose and fell, warming the cold corners of his heart. Geneva's laugh was more full bodied and came deeper from the throat. Lanae's girlish sound reached the cold places he had buried deep inside, melting them like marshmallows in the cocoa Jax and Mia were now drinking.

Sage scanned the turquoise and off-white kitchen, noted the door that undoubtedly led to the attached garage. He stepped toward Lanae's space next to the counter, and almost got stabbed with the knife and pie server she held in one hand. Before they could comment, Lezlie swooped behind Lanae and untied her apron. Moselle took the utensils from Lanae's hand, and said, "I'll serve the cheesecake."

Free of her apron, Lanae ignored Rainn's attempt at getting Geneva's attention. The sisters carried on, something about how much their mother had loved Esther Williams swimming through movies of an older generation.

Lanae finally turned her attention to Sage.

"Is there somewhere we can have some privacy?" Sage bent low to ask Lanae once they were close enough they didn't have to holler.

"The garage is heated. Eric does some woodworking, and Moselle's workbench is there.

Follow me." Lanae reached for his hand and led him through the kitchen to the back door. "It just so happens, he's fixing a couple broken slats on Geneva's porch swing."

She switched on the light before raising the dial on a portable electric heater. The glider was balanced on a couple buckets. They shared a nervous laugh. "Looks like the sawhorses are under the door."

Eric's wood-working was obvious. Birdhouses, mostly made of barn wood, marched in a row on the workbench. Brushes and wood stains and various tools were arranged in rows and shelves above.

Sage drew a deep breath. A stainless steel table saw held court off to one side. The man's place kind of reminded him of his barn.

"The messy side is where Moselle works. The doors used to be in *Frivolities* when she lived in the loft. You get the idea."

He nodded, but he'd heard enough talk about arts and crafts. "I'm going to jump right in. A lot happened in Florida. You could say I came to my senses. I even wrote you a letter. Thanks for the ones you wrote to me."

Lanae relaxed before his eyes, softened as though she lost her starch. "So you found them. I struggled. Doubted whether I should leave them for you. I didn't know if you'd want to hear what's in my heart."

Sage rested his hands on her shoulders. She looked up and sighed when their gazes met. "Thanks. I'll always savor your words to me. My letter for you is out in my truck, I'll give it to you later. Uncle Ted claims lovers always write letters, even if they're nothing more than 'remember the dry cleaning.'"

"Or, 'feed the horses for me?'" Lanae slid her

hands around his waist and hugged Sage as though she never wanted to let him go. "I can hardly wait to read the words you wrote to me. I imagine it was scary opening up your heart like that."

"I doubt you can imagine what it was like when I started to feel. I'd become used to wallowing in a dark place, avoiding emotions. It was scary because I wondered what you would expect compared to what I thought Becca expected of me. I wanted to make Becca happy. I couldn't."

Lanae shook her head. "A person has to make his or her own happiness."

"That's what she told me. She claimed it wasn't my job to make her happy."

"Joy is found in the Lord, Sage. He supplies us with all our essential needs. He gives us His creation and other people for our pleasure, and I believe to please Himself."

"I used to think He provided people to fulfill each other."

"To a certain extent, I suppose that's true. I wasn't quite prepared when I met you and was hit with the way you made me yearn. I was more determined to go after what I wanted than I was scared of the way I felt about you."

"Glad you wanted me. We've got a lot to iron out here. Please have a seat, and if it gets too uncomfortable, you can sit on my lap," he said with a smile.

She looked like her heart was in her hazel eyes. Lanae took his hand in both of hers and sat sideways on the glider swing so she could face him.

Sage made sure they could sit without falling, then tried to do the same. He settled for angling his back in the corner. "The first time I saw you, you sparkled. I didn't know it then, but you were about to draw me out of my dark corner of the world into your spark for life."

"When I first saw you, your calm cowboy way took my breath. You are in your element out there in the country."

"I wanted to be left alone in the country. Didn't know what to think when Lezlie told me she'd invited you to come out riding. I was interested in you from the get-go, but I fought it. Then when you told me about having been sick..." He cocked his head to the left. "...that threw me and I stepped way back from being attracted to you."

"When I found the letters, I couldn't let the past alone. I don't know why exactly, but I felt for Kate. I couldn't understand why you weren't more excited, ready to dig into the mystery with me."

"I thought I needed to keep buried the secret of Uncle Ted and Granddad."

"I can see that now. When I started falling for you, I got so frustrated because you wouldn't move on with your own life. When you said you still loved Becca, I pictured my heart splintering. I realized what I had been missing by not having someone to share my life with. When I saw you weeping over Becca, my heart was tattered and torn."

He hadn't meant to hurt her. "You misunderstood. I was saying good-bye."

He leaned in and brushed her cheek with his lips. *So soft.*

"When we first met, I missed my wife as much as I had when she first died. You made me feel again. I didn't like facing those emotions. You made me wonder about sharing life with a woman again. You are so full of life, Lanae, but I fought those feelings. I kind of got locked into loving my horses again. Loving horses is safe."

"Unless you get bucked off."

They shared laughter. Sage drew her close, making the swing tip. He balanced it again by planting his foot.

He smoothed his hand over her soft, short hair. "I'll never forget the way you fell in that mud and then wallowed in it like a kid. Your zest made it next to impossible for me to walk away."

"And being in the country again, feeling your connection with the land, I wanted the whole enchilada. But you mixed me all up, pulling me close and pushing me away at the same time."

"You wanted to get answers. I needed to keep Uncle Ted's identity hidden. I thought I could distract you, but it didn't work. My life was distracted, filled with you."

"I'm sorry. I got so obsessed over the letters. I got sidetracked from the rest of life because of the mystery—"

"I couldn't make sense of the way you insisted on invading someone else's privacy. Especially when it became Tippin family privacy and Uncle Ted's secret."

"I was wrong, Sage. My motivation was right in that I wanted to show you how to enjoy what you have. I wanted you to know you could live each day as though it's your last instead of focusing on the loss of Becca."

"There came a point when you replaced my thoughts of Becca." He wanted to be done with words, to go on with the notion of living a full life, together.

Lanae looked like she was busting with more to say.

"I was projecting my own discontent in pointing out where I thought you were going wrong. I had no business butting in on God's job of changing your outlook. It's so not up to any individual to point out the wrong in another's attitude."

"But I needed that."

She went on as though he hadn't agreed. "So wrapped up in the past, I forgot to focus on living for today myself. I admit while pointing a finger at you, I was as bad as you were, Sage, living in the past. I kept thinking about the ranch and decided I wasn't happy with my life. I wanted to live in the country again."

"God used it all anyway, and we can give Him the glory for any changes for the good. I feel like a man with a new lease on life."

"Isn't it something, the way we can get so caught up that we forget to live to bring God glory?" Sage wrapped his arms around Lanae, braced his foot on the floor so the seat was secure with his movement, and breathed her in. He thanked God for bringing her into his life.

"The truth, rather than secrets and lies. Truth comes from God and the devil denies truth." Lanae spoke the words he was thinking.

Sage loosened his hold.

Lanae took advantage and lifted her hand to his face. She ran her fingertips over his cheekbone and, followed the ridge of his crooked nose with one fingertip. Finally, she kissed him so lightly he wondered if he imagined the brush of her lips.

He ran his hands down her arms, making her elbows bend so he could clasp her hands. He punctuated each word with a kiss somewhere on her face. "I. Did. Not. Want. To. Feel. I couldn't bring myself to even think about risking hurt again."

Following the delicate touches of lips to soft face, he gave her a playful, teasing kiss. "When we're alone I only want to hold you. That would get in the way of getting to know you better."

"Wow. I respect your strength for restraint. Think we can pull that off?" She pecked him on the nose.

He wanted her to come alongside and go with him anywhere. "I've sensed this fire between us since we first met."

"You had me when I saw you in your cowboy hat. I thought at times you were more than a little attracted. And, all I wanted was for you to kiss me. And now, I never want you to stop!"

"Sounds like a good idea." He caught her chin and tilted her face up so he could look into her ever-changing hazel eyes.

Her invitation drew him in, tossed out some of his restraint. He leaned down, watched her pupils dilate, the darker blue rim joining the green. She smelled like the sweetest freshness imaginable. Like vanilla and sugar and spring grass. Lanae.

His Lanae.

His thumb started an adventure of discovery as it traced her fine-boned features. He let his eyes drift shut, inhaling her scent.

All woman, his Lanae.

His eyes shot open. He reared back.

His throat thickened and he gruffly cleared it. "You are mine, sweet Lanae."

He moved close and sealed that pact with a kiss that seared. They belonged to no one but each other.

With effort, he released their connection. "The first time I touched you I wanted to jump right in and cling for all it's worth. Then I was afraid to take advantage of a willing woman."

"I've been willing since we met, Sage." Lanae's voice was a hoarse whisper. She choked out a laugh. "Talk about willpower."

"I don't know what there is about you that I find so irresistible, but you're so fresh and female. Quite a treat after life spent mostly in the company of animals."

"Sage, you're killing me," she moaned.

Lost in the moment, he continued to journey over Lanae's cheek, so much smoother than Snorty's muzzle.

And he had kissed Snorty's muzzle.

Before he could think about laughing or saying anything, she placed a hand on each side of his head and grabbed him close, targeting his mouth.

Their kiss deepened. Her body sighed closer to his in surrender.

His tension seeped out of the way, to be replaced by a sense of belonging no other human contact had brought.

After some intensity, when he felt her slump even more, Sage ended the kiss by pulling back. He refused to admit he was as shaken by what had happened as she appeared to be. But he loosened his arms so she couldn't feel him quavering.

He wanted a lifetime of this woman shaking him up.

But what if she got sick again?

As if reading his mind, Lanae spoke. "I am not a candidate for cirrhosis, liver failure, or even cancer like

Becca. However, the hepatitis stays in tissues so I can't give blood, for example, but, Sage," she emphasized each word with a tap to his chest. "I. Am. Alive."

"You keep telling me. I know about doctor visits. And I know all about hospice nurses. And that dreaded question, 'What level is your pain today?' My own pain over the inability to help her, to fix things for Becca, drove me crazy. I felt like the thawed-out, bleeding horse probably does just before it's put down. The pain of helplessness hovered just under being unbearable."

"Believe me, I've been down that painful road of uncertainty, and I don't want to revisit that place."

Sage rose to his feet. "Yeah, well, it's kinda hard to trust and love when I remember the hurt. Life isn't safe."

"Sage, love and trust and faith are intertwined. I know whatever I face, the Lord goes with me, right through it."

"I believed God let me down, when all along I'm the one who had let Him down."

"I don't believe in coincidence, Sage. Things happen, life happens, for a reason. And I believe in God's timing. You were meant to advertise your mother's vanity. I was meant to find the letters." She stood.

"We were meant to fall in love," they said at the same time.

Sage pulled her in close, kissed the top of her head. After a moment, she broke the embrace to look up at him. "I don't have to admit to you I've had an aversion to holidays—"

"No kidding?" Lanae said with a wide smile. "Sorry, I'll try not to interrupt again."

"It's OK. About Valentine's Day—if the roads are clear, I'd like to take my turn at giving a party. It's early to the rest of the world, and we could keep the reason for the party to ourselves, but would you consider it an engagement party?"

"Yes, I'll marry you!" Lanae squealed like a five-year-old receiving a tickle. She jumped up and down and twirled the way she had on the acreage.

No doubt about it. Life was grand when you were alive in love.

And choosing peace with Jesus overrides a dark soul.

Sage stilled her with a touch and drew her hand to his lips. He kissed her palm. "That fire you mentioned. We mustn't get burned. Let's throw water on it and rejoin this party, shall we?"

20

For there is nothing hidden that will not be disclosed, and nothing concealed that will not be known, or brought out into the open. —Luke 8:17

Two weeks later, the *Frivolities* women were replacing the vanity display in the window. Lanae said, "I enjoy getting ready for Christmas, but I'm feeling all full of romance. Is it too early to fill the display spot with a Valentine theme?"

"I can tell you're thinking of hearts and flowers. It's so sweet that you and Sage have found one another," Moselle said, smoothing a hand over the framed collage. "How about red and white for now, we can add hearts later."

"We need to give that to Kate and Ted, don't you think?" Geneva nodded at the collage.

"Took the words right out of my mouth, Sis. Moselle," Lanae caught her niece's eye, "would you give me a hand with the vanity? I think we can support the mirror with our shoulders to lift it down."

Moselle used a stool to step onto the display floor, and took hold.

Geneva went to the side to grip the back end, while Lanae took the front. "Okay, we've got the weight, just rest it on the edge, Moselle, then come back down. Ouch!" Geneva screeched.

"What, Mom?"

A loose screw dropped to the floor.

"Set it down." Lanae wove behind Geneva, where a small piece of supporting wood swung loose behind the mirror.

Moselle handed Lanae the screw, and with the other hand, replaced the wood in its vertical position.

"Wait," Geneva said, "what's that?"

Behind the wood, a folded piece of paper came loose from the tape that had disintegrated.

"Another letter?" The women wondered together.

"This time, Sage gets the honor." Lanae said, reaching for her cell phone.

****

Soft instrumental hymns filled the loft while Lanae waited for her love to return to her side. She heard his tread on the backstairs, caught sight of her bright cowboy in the navy and yellow shirt and diamond earring. Filling her vision with Sage's approach now reminded her of observing his movements at Moselle's party. He'd gone for another piece of cheesecake, but Jaxson interrupted to ask a question. The way Sage related to Jaxson filled her with such love, she wanted the honeymoon. He had the patience of Job, as though he could spend a week giving an answer, no matter what was going on.

An outlandish thought struck. She was going to be a mother and a grandmother. Attained through marriage, but what did that matter? She'd have a family of her own.

She waited until he lifted his gaze to meet hers, before unlocking the slider. He leaped onto the deck. The warmth of completion, such love welled up, her ribcage could surely crack wide open. No doubt, he'd need his sage wisdom to connect with the words, whatever they were, written on the paper she found.

Now, wouldn't she feel foolish if it was a simple receipt?

"You look pretty serious," he greeted.

Lord, grant him the perception and sense of King Solomon. "Hi," she managed. Her mouth was dry.

He opened his arms and gave her a smile that promised sunshine the rest of her life. "Kiss first. Then let's see what you found."

Their gazes locked. Before she closed her eyes to meet the softness of his lips, she hoped his unspoken promise of forever mirrored hers.

He released her, but she held onto his hand. *"Give him strength, Lord, whatever he's about to discover."*

Sage held her hand as he reached out.

My Dear Mother,

God has been giving me glimpses of heaven. I need a clean heart before I see Him face to face.

I am so sorry Ted is somewhere far away, taking the blame for a crime he didn't commit. Did you believe Ted is the one who killed Dad?

I don't know why our father was so mean. Can I blame it on the whiskey? No, it may have been an influence, but we make our choices.

The way I chose to help end a wretched life to save my brother.

I heard them yelling from the woods, that Fourth of July

long ago, where Father and Teddy were chopping wood.

When I watched their struggle, Father got the ax away from Ted. The force broke the ax against the bumper of our old car. I ran and picked up the handle when Dad reached for the business end.

Father would have struck Ted.

I was faster. I hit Father in the head.

Ted pulled me close.

When Father moaned, Ted hit him, then pulled me close.

"I'll leave," Teddy said. "Let people believe what they want. At least he'll never hurt anyone again. You were never here, understand? I love you, Vi."

And he was gone.

I cowered behind a cottonwood, all my tears dried up. I listened to the groans. Waiting, for what felt like hours. Finally, Father struggled to his elbow. The devil must have taken over me. I wouldn't let the man find his hands and knees, wouldn't let him hurt anyone ever again.

I ran to the ax handle and swung like I expected a home run. Twice. I finished the job we began together.

Dear Mother, I'm taking the coward's way out by writing this. I'm sorry, I cannot face you.

I will love you always, and I hope you see your beloved Teddy again someday. I did it for him. For all of us.

Our Lord forgave David and called him a man after God's own heart. I don't know about that part as the way God sees me, yet I have made peace. None of us deserve forgiveness, but I know I am forgiven.

I pray you are able to forgive me as well. Someday, your tears of sorrow will be replaced by joy incomparable.

I Love you, Mom.
Violet

"Oh, Sage."

"Yeah. What do you say about knowing your mother had a hand in your grandfather's murder?" He scrubbed a hand over the top of his head then buried his face.

Lanae's reaction was instinctual. She reached out and took the yellowed paper Sage offered. The words of John 15:13 wove through her mind. "Greater love has no one than this, that one lay down his life for his friends."

She went behind the couch, hugged him, then rubbed his neck and shoulders. "None of us were there. None of us know what we would do, if the Lord called us to give our life for another."

He grabbed her hand, guided her onto his lap. "Jesus commands us to love one another and even die, if need be."

"John 15:13 again." She caressed his cheek. "How did your mother, die?"

"A stroke took her immediately."

"He was merciful." She lifted herself up and enfolded his head in her arms, wishing she was large enough to wrap herself around him. To absorb his hurt.

She touched his right brow with one finger. She traced over the other brow, trailed down and felt the prominent cheekbone, the bristles of stubble on his jaw. Over the nose that listed off-center. Her hand becalmed when she finally rested two fingertips on the contour of his chin.

By now, his chest was rising as high and fast as hers, matching her rapid breathing. "You game for a short engagement?"

Her lips parted, but she couldn't speak. She nodded instead.

Sage lifted those two fingers from his chin and kissed them. Then he folded them into his rough textured grasp and settled her palm over his heart.

A whisper before their lips met, he said, "You're mine forever."

"Sage," she whispered.

"Sweet," he said.

They belonged to one another, it was God-ordained. They sealed their promise of forever with another kiss.

Thank you for purchasing this Pelican Book Group / White Rose Publishing title. For other inspirational stories of romance, please visit our on-line bookstore at www.pelicanbookgroup.com.

For questions or more information, contact us at titleadmin@pelicanbookgroup.com.

White Rose Publishing
Where Faith is the Cornerstone of Love™
www.pelicanbookgroup.com

May God's glory shine through
this inspirational work of fiction.

AMDG